JUNIOR MONSTER SCOUTS

4 Books in 1!

ALSO BY JOE McGEE

Night Frights
The Haunted Mustache
The Lurking Lima Bean

JUNIOR MONSTER SCOUTS

4 Books in 1!

The Monster Squad • Crash! Bang! Boo!
It's Raining Bats and Frogs! • Monster of Disguise

By Joe McGee
Illustrated by Ethan Long

ALADDIN

NEW YORK   LONDON   TORONTO   SYDNEY   NEW DELHI

ALADDIN

An imprint of Simon & Schuster Children's Publishing Division
1230 Avenue of the Americas, New York, New York 10020
This Aladdin hardcover edition June 2021
The Monster Squad and *Crash! Bang! Boo!* text copyright © 2019 by Joseph McGee
The Monster Squad and *Crash! Bang! Boo!* illustrations copyright © 2019 by Ethan Long
It's Raining Bats and Frogs! and *Monster of Disguise* text copyright © 2020 by Joseph McGee
It's Raining Bats and Frogs! and *Monster of Disguise* illustrations copyright © 2020 by Ethan Long
Cover illustration copyright © 2019 by Ethan Long
All rights reserved, including the right of reproduction in whole or in part in any form.
ALADDIN and related logo are registered trademarks of Simon & Schuster, Inc.
For information about special discounts for bulk purchases, please contact Simon & Schuster Special Sales at 1-866-506-1949 or business@simonandschuster.com.
The Simon & Schuster Speakers Bureau can bring authors to your live event.
For more information or to book an event contact the Simon & Schuster Speakers Bureau at 1-866-248-3049 or visit our website at www.simonspeakers.com.
Series designed by Karin Paprocki
The illustrations for this book were rendered digitally.
The text of this book was set in Centaur MT.
Manufactured in the United States of America 0521 FFG
2 4 6 8 10 9 7 5 3 1
Library of Congress Control Number 2021935009
ISBN 9781665907576 (hc)
ISBN 9781534436787 (*The Monster Squad* ebook)
ISBN 9781534436817 (*Crash! Bang! Boo!* ebook)
ISBN 9781534436848 (*It's Raining Bats and Frogs!* ebook)
ISBN 9781534436879 (*Monster of Disguise* ebook)
These titles were previously published individually.

· THE SCOUTS ·

VAMPYRA may be a vampire, but that doesn't mean she wants your blood. Gross! In fact, she doesn't even like ketchup! She loves gymnastics, especially cart- wheels, and one of her favorite things is hanging upside down ... even when she's *not* a bat. She loves garlic in her food and sleeps in past noon, preferring the nighttime over the day. She lives in Castle Dracula with her mom, dad (Dracula), and aunts, who are always after her to brush her fangs and clean her cape.

WOLFY and his family live high in the mountains above Castle Dracula, where they can get the best view of the moon. He likes to hike and play in the creek and gaze at the stars. He especially likes to fetch sticks with his dad, Wolf Man, and go on family pack runs, even if he has to put up with all of his little brothers and sisters. They're always howling when he tries to talk! Mom says he has his father's fur. Boy, is he proud of that!

 **FRANKY STEIN** has always been bigger than the other monsters. But it's not just his body that's big. It's his brain and his heart as well. He has plenty of hugs and smiles to go around. His dad, Frankenstein, is the scoutmaster, and one of Franky's favorite things is his well-worn Junior Monster Scout handbook. One day Franky is going to be a scoutmaster, like his dad. But for now . . . he wants a puppy. Dad says he'll make Franky one soon. Mom says Franky has to keep his workshop clean for a week first.

GLOOMY
WOODS

LAKE

VILLAGE

BARON VON
GRUMP'S HOUSE

CONTENTS

The Monster Squad

FOR JESSICA

★ ★ ★ ★

*I will not let you go into
the unknown alone.*
—Bram Stoker

CHAPTER
1

WOLFY TOOK A DEEP BREATH. HE LOOKED to the sky. He leaned way back and let out the biggest, longest, loudest howl he could. It was a very good howl. It was such a good howl that it went right past the forest, over the covered bridge, through the village, and all the way to the Old Windmill.

"That was a good one!" said Franky Stein.

"I'll bet they could hear that howl all the way back at the castle!" said Vampyra.

"Thanks!" said Wolfy. He was very proud of himself. Tonight was the Junior Monster Scout meeting, and Wolfy wanted to earn his Howling Merit Badge.

In fact, Wolfy's howl was such a good howl that it reached right through the open window of the Old Windmill, right into the ears of Baron Von Grump.

Baron Von Grump was always grumpy. Everything about him was grumpy. Even his eyebrows were grumpy. They were like two big, black, bushy, *grumpy* caterpillars crawling across his forehead. They were even blacker than Edgar, his pet crow.

"What was that *noise?*" he sneered. "That sounded like a howl. A *monstrous* howl. Oh, how I despise those wretched monsters!"

Edgar hopped onto the windowsill and peered out over the village. "Caw, caw!" Edgar did not like monsters either.

Baron Von Grump did not like noise. Baron Von Grump did not like anything, really, except for playing his violin and making plans. Baron Von Grump *loved* making plans. He loved that almost as much as he loved playing his violin.

So you see, Baron Von Grump loved *two* things. And everything else, he did not. Okay, he loved Edgar, too. *Three* things. Baron Von Grump loved three things.

Baron Von Grump looked out his window and glared at the village. Edgar glared with him.

Today was the village cheese festival, and all of the villagers were busy setting up.

"Look at them!" he said. "Smiling, talking, singing, why . . . they're even chewing gum! I cannot stand when people chew gum . . . or sing, or talk, or smile. These villagers are almost as bad as those miserable monsters."

See? Baron Von Grump did not like anything besides making plans and his violin
and Edgar. With all of this noise Baron Von
Grump could not concentrate. If he could
not concentrate, he could not play his violin. If he could not play his violin, he would

become even grumpier than the grump he already was. And *that* is a lot of grump.

"I have a plan!" he said with a sly smirk.

"Caw! Caw!" said Edgar.

A plan! This made Baron Von Grump happy for one half of a second.

Make a smile. Just a little one. Barely twitch the corners of your mouth. Now stop. That was how long Baron Von Grump was happy. That was not very long, was it?

Edgar hopped onto Baron Von Grump's shoulder.

Baron Von Grump slammed his shutters closed. He knew just what to do to get rid of all of those smiling, talking, singing, gum-chewing villagers. He knew just how to chase them away.

CHAPTER
2

JUST AS WOLFY WAS GETTING READY to howl again, he heard something. He stopped. He listened. Wolfy was a very good listener. He had ears like a wolf.

It sounded like someone was crying. It did not sound like a good cry, like when you get a new puppy or some ice cream and you're so happy that you cry. No, this sounded like a sad cry.

"Hey," said Wolfy, "I hear someone."

Wolfy followed the sound of crying. Vampyra and Franky went with him. The crying led them down past the graveyard, along the crooked trail, and right to the edge of the Gloomy Woods. A little boy sat by the side of the trail. It was Peter, the piper, from the village. He was crying into his hat.

"What's wrong?" asked Wolfy.

Peter jumped. "Don't eat me!"

The junior monsters looked confused.

Stop reading and look at the nearest person. Now say, "Don't eat me!" They look confused, don't they? They are probably giving you a funny look. That is the kind of look the junior monsters gave Peter.

"Why would we eat you?" asked Vampyra.

"Because you're monsters," said Peter. "Monsters eat people, right?"

"We're friendly monsters," said Franky.

"Friendly monsters?" Peter asked. "The stories don't say anything about *friendly* monsters."

"That's just it," said Vampyra. She swished her cape. "They're only *stories!*"

"My dad says Baron Von Grump made up all of those stories about us," said Franky. "And everyone believed him."

"Well, you're certainly not scary, like in the stories," said Peter. "I've never met a real monster before."

"We're not just monsters. We are Junior Monster *Scouts*!" said Wolfy. "Why are you crying?"

"I was playing a song on my flute, and when I turned around, my Shadow was gone!" Peter said.

"Cheer up," said Franky. "We'll find your shadow!" He looked behind a bush. He looked under a rock. "Have you checked your pockets? Oh, hey, I found it! Look, there it is!" He pointed to Peter's shadow stretched out next to him.

"Not *that* shadow," said Peter. "My kitten. *Her* name is Shadow." He started to cry again.

Peter was very sad.

Wolfy, Vampyra, and Franky did not like seeing anyone sad.

"Don't worry," said Wolfy. "We'll help you find Shadow."

"You will?" said Peter. He wiped his tears away.

"We sure will," said Franky.

"By paw or claw, by tooth or wing, Junior Monster Scouts can do anything!" said Vampyra.

CHAPTER
3

"WE'LL FIND SHADOW BY FOLLOWING her scent," said Wolfy. He pointed to his nose. "I am very good at sniffing things out."

"Shadow likes to sleep in my hat," said Peter. "Maybe that will help."

Wolfy sniffed Peter's hat. He sniffed the air. He sniffed the ground. He sniffed the air again.

"Do you have anything that belongs to Shadow?" asked Wolfy.

"I have her favorite toy," said Peter. He held out a little stuffed mouse.

Wolfy sniffed that, too. "Aha!" he said.

He had Shadow's scent, and he had the trail. But he did not like where it led.

"Shadow went in there," he said. He pointed to the Gloomy Woods.

Peter gulped.

Franky shivered.

Vampyra squeezed her eyes shut.

The Gloomy Woods was dark, and spooky, and very, very gloomy. That's why it was called the Gloomy Woods.

You might think that monsters would like dark, spooky, and very, very gloomy things. But that is just another *story*. They only like kind of gloomy things, not very, *very* gloomy.

"It won't be so bad if we go in together," said Wolfy. He took one step toward the woods. He was nervous.

"I have an idea," said Vampyra. "I know a way to make the Gloomy Woods not so gloomy."

"How?" asked Franky. "I don't think anything can make it less gloomy."

"Peter," said Vampyra, "did you say you play the flute?"

"I do," said Peter. "I can play lots of songs!"

"Well, then why don't you play us a song?" asked Vampyra.

Peter picked up his flute and played a song. It was a cheery, happy song. It worked! They all felt a little better, a

little braver, and a lot less gloomy.

"Lead the way, Peter!" said Franky.

Wolfy, Franky, and Vampyra followed Peter into the Gloomy Woods.

CHAPTER 4

BARON VON GRUMP COVERED HIS EARS.
He growled. He groaned. He grimaced. *Why
is everyone so loud? And happy?* Why, he'd
even heard a villager say "Good morning" to
another villager just a minute ago.

Every villager was out and about, young
and old, waving their little cheese flags, and
wearing hats made of cheese wheels. There
was even a parade and a wagon piled high
with cheese. White cheese, yellow cheese,

pink cheese, cheese with holes. Square cheese, round cheese. Cheese, cheese, cheese, CHEESE!

"They are driving me crazy with all of their noise!" he said to Edgar. "How am I supposed to practice my violin with them making such a racket? And oh, the stench! The horrible, terrible stink of their cheeses."

Baron Von Grump pinched his nose shut with a clothespin. "Bud I hab a plan. I doh justh whut to do!"

"Caw! Caw!" said Edgar.

Baron Von Grump went down, down, down the sagging staircase of the Old Windmill, all the way to the basement. Edgar flew down the stairs, leading the way. Baron Von Grump hardly ever went down to the basement. He lived in the top room of the very old, very rickety, very crooked windmill. The basement was dark, and damp, and filled with rats. Big, hairy black rats with long pink tails and bright red eyes.

Baron Von Grump lit a candle. The rats blinked. There were a lot of rats. There was a lot of blinking.

"Hey," said a very big rat, munching on a wedge of cheese, "put that candle out!"

The rats did not like light very much.

"How would you like all the cheese you could eat?" asked Baron Von Grump.

The rats liked cheese a lot. They liked cheese *more* than they disliked light. The

rats listened to what Baron Von Grump had to say. Baron Von Grump said that there was a lot of cheese in the village. He said that each house was filled with cheese. He also said that the rats could have *all* of it . . . as long as they chased the villagers away. And chewed their cheese *quietly*.

"Hmm," said the big rat. "I'll put it to a vote."

The big rat called all of the other rats together and explained Baron Von Grump's offer. The rats thought this was a very good idea. Unfortunately, the village was much brighter than the basement of the Old Windmill, but the village was also filled with cheese.

"We'll do it!" said the big rat. He swallowed his wedge of cheese. He burped. He did not have very nice manners.

Baron Von Grump smiled. It was a very small smile, a crooked smile, certainly not a full smile. But it was something.

Edgar's beady little black eyes seemed to smile as well.

"Soon," said Baron Von Grump, "those villagers will be gone, and I'll finally have some peace and quiet. I will finally be able to play my violin without all of their cheering and chattering and cheese stink!"

CHAPTER

5

THE GLOOMY WOODS WAS VERY, VERY dark. It was so dark that Wolfy, Vampyra, Franky, and Peter could barely see their own hands in front of their own faces.

The Gloomy Woods was also filled with trees. Lots and lots of trees to walk right into. Or roots to trip you up. The Gloomy Woods was a dangerous place.

"Ouch!" said Peter. A branch knocked his hat off.

"Oof!" said Franky. He stumbled over a log.

Wolfy and Vampyra did not stumble or hit anything. Werewolves and vampires can see in the dark. But that did not help Peter and Franky.

"We need to help them," said Vampyra.

"We can be their eyes," said Wolfy.

Wolfy held Peter's hand. Vampyra held Franky's hand. Now they could walk through the Gloomy Woods.

Wolfy sniffed the air.

"Shadow is close!" he said.

"She might be scared of you at first, like I was," said Peter.

"She might hide from us," said Franky.

"I think Peter can help with that," said Vampyra. "His music helped us feel not so

gloomy. Maybe he can help Shadow feel not so gloomy."

"Good idea," said Peter. He took out his flute and played another song.

When he was finished with his song, he put his flute away. The junior monsters waited and listened. A soft meow came from somewhere in front of them. In front of them and *above* them.

"Did you hear something?" asked Franky.

"That's Shadow!" said Peter.

"Meow!"

"Shadow is in one of these trees!" said Wolfy.

"Which one?" Peter asked. But he could not even see one tree, let alone the tree that Shadow was in. Close your eyes. Close them tight. Now look for a kitten. You can't see one, right? You can't see anything. That's how dark it was.

"I think I know a way to find out which tree Shadow is in," said Vampyra.

CHAPTER

6

THE VILLAGE WAS FILLED WITH RATS.

Big rats, short rats, thin rats, long rats. Rats scampered down the streets. They crawled into houses through windows. They slid under doors. They hopped onto roofs and dropped down the chimneys. They twitched their pink tails and grinned with their yellow teeth. The rats ran *everywhere* . . . and everywhere they ran, the villagers ran too.

"This is great!" said the rats. "So much cheese!"

Now, mind you, the rats were not hurting anyone. They certainly did not want to *overly* upset the villagers. All they wanted was cheese, and Baron Von Grump had been right. There was a lot of cheese in this village! But the villagers did not know what the rats wanted. The villagers did not stop to ask the rats why they had come in through the windows and down the chimneys, and why they were on the village streets.

The villagers just ran in circles. They climbed atop wagons. They stood on chairs.

"There are too many of them!" said a villager.

"We'll never get rid of them all!" said another.

"They're eating our cheese!" cried a third villager.

"Everyone!" said the mayor, shouting through a very loud bullhorn. "Gather your things. Pack your bags. Collect your children. We must leave the village!"

Baron Von Grump clapped his hands together. He leaned out of his window and watched.

"My plan is working!" he said. "Soon those cheese-eating, song-singing, gum-chewing, happy villagers will be gone and I'll be able to play, play, play my violin without any distraction!"

He spun in a circle, jumped up, and clicked his heels together. Edgar sat on the edge of a rafter and bobbed his head up and down.

"Caw! Caw!"

"Yes, my friend," said Baron Von Grump, "the sooner the better." He did not like the villagers' panicked hollering and shouting, and he certainly did not like the mayor's bullhorn.

Baron Von Grump slammed his shutters closed again. He stomped to his favorite chair, sat down, and opened his violin case. He blew off the dust and the cobwebs and lifted the violin to his chin.

He placed the bow on the strings.

He took a deep breath, closed his eyes, and drew the bow across the strings.

It made a terrible screech.

"Caw! Caw!" shrieked Edgar. He flew straight to the window . . . and into the closed shutters.

"Well, of course it's not tuned!" growled Baron Von Grump, waving his bow. "How

am I supposed to tune it when I can't even hear myself think?!"

Edgar shrugged his wings. Baron Von Grump shoved his violin back into the case and slapped the lid closed.

7

SINCE VAMPYRA WAS A VAMPIRE, SHE had a few special powers. One of her powers was being able to turn into a bat. If Vampyra turned into a bat, she could see better in the dark *and* she could fly up to the tops of the trees to see which one Shadow was in.

Wolfy, Franky, and Peter thought this was a very good idea.

"Meow."

So did Shadow.

Vampyra closed her eyes. She wrapped her cape around her body. She counted, "One . . . two . . . three." And then POOF! Vampyra turned into a bat.

She fluttered and flapped and flittered around the others. Being a bat was fun! She was close to earning her Junior Monster Scout Flying Merit Badge.

"Do you see her yet?" asked Peter.

"Not yet!" said Vampyra.

Vampyra flew up above their heads. She flew higher and higher, and soon she was at the top branches. It was even darker up there! There were lots of branches and lots of leaves.

But as a bat, Vampyra could see even better.

"Meow, meow," said Shadow.

Vampyra was getting close. She soared and swooped and flew around the branches and treetops.

"I see her!" she said. Vampyra flapped her wings and got closer. Sure enough, Shadow was curled up on a branch right over their heads. "You certainly do look like a shadow," Vampyra said to the little black kitten. "I almost didn't see you."

Shadow arched her back and stared at Vampyra the bat, and then at the ground. She hissed. She blinked her green eyes. She wanted to jump, but it was too far and she was scared.

"It's okay," said Vampyra. She flashed her best batty smile. "We'll help you get down."

"Meow, meow."

Vampyra flapped back down to her friends. She fluttered in the air, and her wings became her cape, and one . . . two . . . three . . . her body changed from bat to girl.

"Wow!" said Peter. "I wish I could do that!"

"Did you find her?" asked Wolfy.

"I did," said Vampyra. "Shadow is right above us. But it's too far for her to jump, too high for us to reach, and I'm too little a bat to carry her."

Franky scratched his head. He twisted his bolts. He'd listened hard to what Vampyra had said. Franky was a very good listener.

"Too high to reach?" he asked.

"I'm afraid so," said Vampyra.

"Maybe not for *all* of us," said Franky.

CHAPTER
8

BARON VON GRUMP WAITED. HE LISTENED. He waited and listened. No one was hollering. No one was shouting. No one was singing or saying, "Good morning." No one was shouting, "RATS!" And there was certainly no bullhorn.

"Could it be?" asked Baron Von Grump. "Could those irksome villagers finally be gone?"

"Caw, caw!" said Edgar.

"Yes! Yes, my fine feathered friend," said Baron Von Grump, "let us see for ourselves."

He stomped over to his shutters. He pushed them wide open. He raised his big,

black, bushy eyebrows. And then Baron Von Grump did something that Baron Von Grump rarely ever did.

Baron Von Grump smiled. Not a small, crooked smile like before. This was a full, wide, genuine smile.

He looked to the left. He looked to the right. He looked across the village.

"They're gone!" he said. He clapped his hands together and danced in a little circle. "The villagers have all gone. My rat plan was a success!"

There were no villagers. No horses. No wagons. No children. No chickens. No smiling or singing or gum-chewing or "good mornings." The village was entirely empty... except for the rats.

Big, fat, lazy rats with wedges of cheese, as far as the eye could see.

Baron Von Grump leaned out his window and shouted down to the rats, "Hey! Would you mind nibbling your cheese just a bit more *quietly*?"

"Sure thing, boss," said the big rat. "HEY! RATS! QUIET DOWN!"

Baron Von Grump's smile disappeared. Rats had been part of his plan. *Loud*, nibbling, cheese-chomping rats had not.

CHAPTER
9

FRANKY STRETCHED HIS LONG ARMS. He stretched his long legs. He stood on his tippy toes and felt around. His fingers touched the bottom branch, but Shadow was still too high up.

Stand up and stretch as high as you can. Put your arms way up over your head. Now wiggle your fingers about. Can you feel a kitten? No, you cannot. That's how Franky felt.

"We'll never be able to reach her," said Peter.

"Never say 'never' when friends work together!" said Franky. "Wolfy, climb onto my shoulders."

Wolfy climbed up and reached for Shadow. But they were still not high enough.

"Vampyra, can you climb onto Wolfy's shoulders?" asked Franky.

Vampyra climbed up. But they were still not tall enough.

"We're so close!" said Vampyra.

"Okay, Peter. Your turn," said Franky. "Be careful!"

"But it's so high up!" said Peter.

"I'll hold your legs," said Vampyra.

"And I'll keep us steady," said Franky.

"We won't let you fall," said Wolfy. "A Junior Monster Scout is always careful and kind."

"Well, okay, then," said Peter. He climbed

up Franky, up Wolfy, and up onto Vampyra's shoulders.

"A little to the left," said Peter. "A little more. Almost there . . ."

Peter's fingers touched soft fur.

"That's it!" said Peter.

"Meow," said Shadow.

Peter gently lifted Shadow off the branch and climbed back down.

He stepped off Vampyra's shoulders and onto Wolfy's head.

"Owwwww!" howled Wolfy.

"Sorry!" Peter said.

Shadow squirmed in Peter's hand.

Peter stepped off Wolfy's head and onto Franky's bolts.

"Yeowch!" Franky hollered.

"Didn't mean that," said Peter.

Shadow arched her back. Peter held her tight and slid down off Franky.

"That was a challenge!" Peter said.

"You're telling me," grumbled Wolfy, rubbing his head.

Once they were all back on the ground, the black kitten jumped right onto Peter's head and curled up under his hat.

"I'm so glad you're safe, Shadow!" said Peter. "I was scared that you'd stay lost."

"Meow," said Shadow. She had been scared too.

But they were still in the Gloomy Woods, and that made them *all* a little scared.

"Maybe we should get out of here," said Wolfy.

Everyone thought that was a very good idea.

Since Wolfy and Vampyra could see better in the dark, they led the group out of the Gloomy Woods. It felt good to be back in the sun, even for Vampyra, who preferred to sleep in during the day and stay up later at night.

But little did they know that while they'd been helping Peter to rescue Shadow, things had gone crazy in the village!

Peter and the Junior Monster Scouts could not believe what they saw. Everyone was leaving the village! Horses and wagons and people with packs and bags and baskets and suitcases marched down the road *away* from the village and away from the Gloomy Woods and the Junior Monster Scouts. They were taking the road toward the lake, and they were sure in a hurry. It was a long, long line of frantic villagers, with the mayor at the front, leading them all with his bullhorn, on his bicycle.

"Hurry!" the mayor shouted through his bullhorn. "Run! Run for your lives! Orderly running, please. No pushing or shoving!"

But everyone pushed and shoved. They were running for their lives!

(Which is kind of silly because the rats weren't hurting anyone at all.)

"Where is everyone going?" asked Wolfy.

"I don't know," said Peter. "Today is the village cheese festival! Let's go find out."

"But they're all the way down the road," said Vampyra.

"We'll never catch them!" said Franky.

"And the mayor's bullhorn is so loud," said Peter. "They won't hear us calling them."

Shadow wiggled out from under Peter's hat. She landed on her feet (cats always land on their feet) and curled around Vampyra's legs.

"I think she likes you," said Peter.

Then Shadow arched her back, straightened her tail, and let out the loudest "Meow" she could. It was very tiny and very cute, but not loud enough to be heard over the shouting, pushing, shoving, and bullhorn.

However, it *did* give Wolfy an idea.

"That's it!" said Wolfy. "Thanks, Shadow! I

know just how to get the villagers' attention."

Wolfy leaned way, way, way back and let out the loudest howl he could.

It worked! The villagers stopped pushing and shoving, and the mayor rode his bicycle back to Peter and the Junior Monster Scouts.

"Where is everyone going?" Peter asked.

The mayor explained the rat problem to them. "And so you see," said the mayor, "we have to leave. They're everywhere! Nibbling our crackers, chomping our cheese, jumping onto our pillows, and climbing our walls. There are too many of them. We have no choice! Oh, woe is us!"

Peter held up his flute.

"I think we might be able to help," he said.

CHAPTER
10

PETER'S PLAN WAS SIMPLE.

First they brought Shadow into the village. As soon as she crawled out from under Peter's hat, she saw the rats. And the rats saw her. Rats do not like kittens. Kittens do not like rats.

Of course, there were other cats in the village. But the village cats were old, and lazy, and not at all interested in chasing around big, cheese-eating rats. Not when the cats could curl up in the sun and swish their tails about.

But Shadow was young, and full of energy, and *very* much interested in chasing a bunch of cheese-eating rats.

The rats dropped their cheese wedges. Shadow hissed. The rats shrieked. Baron Von Grump had *not* mentioned anything about a kitten to the rats. He had promised cheese, and lots of it. But he had failed to mention anything about a spitting, biting, scratching kitten. And what if she woke up the rest of the older lazy, napping cats? What then? No way!

"Run for your lives!" the big rat yelled. Then he burped. He really didn't have any manners at all.

Rats hopped out of windows. They scurried up chimneys. They ran under doors and along rooftops. Everywhere they ran, Shadow followed, darting left and right, right and left. She chased them all in one direction . . . *out* of the village.

Shadow did not really want to catch any of the rats. This was just a fun game for her. But the rats didn't know this, and the rats were scared. There was a lot of pushing and shoving as the rats fled for their lives.

"I feel bad for them," said Wolfy. "All they wanted was cheese."

"They look pretty scared," said Vampyra.

"I have an idea," said Franky. He leaned over and whispered into Peter's ear.

Franky was not telling secrets. That would have been rude. Rats have very good hearing, and Franky didn't want the rats to know what the Junior Monster Scouts were up to. Franky was quite clever.

Peter grinned. "That is a very good idea," he said.

He picked up his flute and played. It was a happy song. It was the kind of song that might make you think of ice cream, and your favorite toy, and warm, fuzzy blankets. When the rats heard it, they felt happy. Very happy. Even the big, burping rat with no manners was happy.

The rats were so happy that they stopped running. They stopped pushing and shoving. They formed one line of happy, smiling rats, following Peter and his flute.

"It's working!" said Wolfy.

"But where should we lead them?" Franky asked. "Where can *they* be happy too?"

"I know!" said Vampyra. "There's plenty of

room in the castle! I'm sure my mom and dad won't mind. We have a great big basement with more than enough room for all of these rats. They can even have Ping-Pong tournaments!"

Peter played his flute and followed Vampyra, Franky, and Wolfy to Dracula's castle. The rats followed Peter. Shadow followed the rats. It was a very long line.

They crossed the drawbridge over the moat. They marched into the castle. They went down, down, down into the basement. Then Peter stopped playing.

"Here you go," said Vampyra to the rats. "You can stay here for as long as you like."

She was right. There was lots of room! And lots of dark places and lots of

cobwebs. It was perfect for a rat.

"Thank you!" said the big rat.

Well, maybe he had *some* manners.

"What's this? What's going on?" said Vampyra's dad from the basement steps.

"Where did all these rats come from?"

"From the village," said Franky.

"They needed a place to stay," said Wolfy, "and they can't stay in the village."

"And our basement is so big," said Vampyra. "Please, Dad? Please, can they stay?"

"Well, I don't see why not," said Vampyra's dad. "But no scampering around at all hours of the day!" he said to the rats. "I need my beauty sleep."

"You—you're *Dracula*," said Peter. "Like, in the stories. You're a *real* monster!"

"What? No!" said Dracula. He popped out one of his pointy teeth. "These aren't even real. See?" He waved it around. "Fake!"

"Then why do you wear them?" Peter asked.

Dracula shrugged. "Good question."

BARON VON GRUMP'S SMILE HAD GONE from a big grin to a little twitch, to a thin line, to a frown. A full, frumpy, sour frown.

Baron Von Grump was angry. He was so angry that he hopped up and down. He stomped his feet. He wrinkled his eyebrows. He even shook his fist in the air and yelled, "I am so angry!"

"Caw! Caw!" said Edgar.

Edgar was angry too.

First it had been the villagers. Then it had been those cheese-nibbling rats. And then, when things had finally gone quiet, when he'd finally picked his violin back up and set the bow against the strings so that he could tune it, someone had howled. A long, loud, rolling howl. Then a kitten. A hissing, spitting kitten. Then there had been a boy with a flute. No, a boy *playing* a flute, and three little monsters all smiling and, and, and . . . *breathing*! Breathing can be very, very loud.

Everything was loud to Baron Von Grump. His own breathing was loud. His hollering, hopping, and stomping was loud. He could barely hear himself think.

With the rats gone, the villagers would move back in. With the villagers back, there would be more smiling, and singing, and gum-chewing, and "good mornings." There would be laughing and breathing and good cheer.

"I am so angry!" roared Baron Von Grump, pacing and stomping around.

See? He was really, really angry.

Think of some time when you were really angry. Think of when you had to go to bed early, or eat lima beans, or clean up your toys *before* you could go out and play. That probably made you angry, right? Well, Baron Von Grump was even angrier than that! Like, a hundred times angrier. Maybe a zillion times.

"Caw! Caw!" said Edgar.

"Stop cawing!" hollered Baron Von Grump. He shook his fist at Edgar and stomped some more.

Edgar's little eyes twinkled mischievously. "Caw?" He flew up to the top rafter

65

and stayed out of Baron Von Grump's way.

"Argh!" yelled Baron Von Grump. He stuffed cotton into his ears and slammed his shutters closed.

That was how angry he was.

CHAPTER
12

THE VILLAGERS, HOWEVER, WERE NOT angry. They were very happy to be back home in their village. They were so happy that they gathered right in the village square, every one of them, from young to old.

There was lots of smiling, lots of sing-ing, and lots of good cheer. There was even lots of gum-chewing. These villagers really liked gum.

After the rats were settled, Franky, Wolfy,

and Vampyra walked Peter back to the village. Everyone was gathered in the square.

"Peter," said the mayor, "you led the rats out of the village. You saved the day! I want to give you a medal."

Peter was proud. "Thank you," he said. "But . . ."

"But what?" said the mayor.

"But I didn't do it alone," said Peter. He called his friends over. "Wolfy, Vampyra, and Franky all helped me. We saved the day together!"

"Don't forget Shadow," said Wolfy.

"Meow," said Shadow.

"But . . . but they're monsters!" said one of the villagers. He hid behind a wagon.

"Monsters are scary," said another villager. She grabbed a pitchfork.

"Don't eat me!" said a third villager. He pulled his hat down over his face.

"They won't eat you," said Peter. "And they're *not* scary. These are nice monsters, and they're my friends. These Junior Monster Scouts helped me find Shadow, and then they helped me lead the rats out of the village."

"Monsters?" said the mayor. *"Helping?"*

"By tooth or wing, by paw or claw, a Junior Monster Scout does it all!" said Vampyra, Franky, and Wolfy all together.

"But they live in the old castle!" said one of the villagers.

"Technically, I live in the mountains *near* the castle," mumbled Wolfy.

"Beyond the Gloomy Woods," said another villager.

"Up past the graveyard!" said a third villager.

"And they're terribly frightening!" said the mayor. "It says so right here!"

He held up a large book. The title was *The Big Book of Scary Monsters*.

"Those are just stories!" said Peter.

"They are?" said the mayor and the villagers.

"Those stories aren't real," said Vampyra.

"They're not?" said the mayor and the villagers.

"We're just like you," said Wolfy. "Maybe just furrier."

"And really quite friendly," said Franky.

"Junior Monster Scouts, you say?" said the mayor.

"That's right," said Vampyra. "We help people."

"And take care of the environment," said Wolfy.

"And learn new things!" said Franky.

The mayor scrunched up his eyebrows. He twisted his mustache. He looked from the book to the monsters, and then back to the book. A smile spread across his face and he tossed the book into a nearby haystack.

"Well, it sounds to me like we need four medals!" declared the mayor.

"Don't forget Shadow," said Franky.

"Meow," said Shadow.

"Five medals," said the mayor.

"Three cheers for the Junior Monster Scouts!" said Peter.

"Hip, hip, hooray!" shouted the villagers. "Hip, hip, hooray! Hip, hip, HOORAY!"

13

AFTER THE CELEBRATION, WOLFY, VAMPYRA, and Franky said good-bye to Peter and Shadow.

"We have to get home," said Wolfy.

"Tonight is our Junior Monster Scout meeting," said Franky.

"But we'll be sure to visit you!" said Vampyra.

They crossed the covered bridge that led out of the village. They passed the Gloomy

Woods. They climbed the hill where Wolfy had practiced his howling. They marched past the old graveyard and back to Castle Dracula just in time to grab their Junior Monster Scout merit badge sashes and make it to their scout meeting.

"So, what did you do today?" asked Franky's dad, Frankenstein.

Wolfy, Vampyra, and Franky took turns telling about how they had helped Peter find Shadow and about leading the rats out of the village.

"And into my basement," mumbled Dracula.

"That sounds like great teamwork!" said Wolfy's dad, Wolf Man. "I think you three earned your Teamwork Merit Badge!"

"Really?" asked Wolfy.

"We did?" asked Franky and Vampyra.

Frankenstein opened the Junior Monster Scout handbook. "You worked together to do something you could not have done individually. Wolfy, you led everyone through the woods to Shadow."

"Vampyra, you flew up and found the branch she was on," said Wolf Man.

"And, Franky, you used your head and your height so that you all could get Shadow out of the tree," said Dracula.

"On top of that, all three of you made a new friend. A human friend. Congratulations, junior monsters," said Frankenstein. He pinned their new badges onto their uniforms.

"One more thing," said Dracula. "Wolfy, that was a great howl. I heard it all the way from the top of my castle!"

"Sounds like someone earned their Howling Merit Badge!" said Wolf Man.

Wolfy and Wolf Man leaned way, way, way back and howled at the moon. Dracula, Frankenstein, Franky, and Vampyra joined in.

"Now let's say the Junior Monster Scout oath," said Frankenstein.

The junior monsters held hands and said together, "I promise to be nice, not scary. To help, not harm. To always try to do my best. I am a monster, but I am not mean. I am a Junior Monster *Scout!*"

CHAPTER
14

BARON VON GRUMP GLARED OUT HIS window. He grumped and he glared. He glared and he grumped.

Edgar perched on his shoulder and glared as well.

"Junior Monster Scouts," he grumbled.

"Caw-caw caw-caw caw," grumbled Edgar.

Baron Von Grump put his eye to his telescope and peered out over the village, over

the covered bridge, beyond the Gloomy Woods, past the old graveyard, and to the top of the hill. There, in the great stone castle, *Dracula's* castle, the monsters were celebrating. They were celebrating how they had foiled him. Him, Baron Von Grump! That would never do.

Why, the monsters were the very reason Baron Von Grump had never been recognized for his musical talent! Ever since that day when he was just a young lad, onstage at the village talent show, prepared to play the song he had practiced over and over and over so that he might win the trophy . . . those meddling monsters had come in and scared everyone. Scared him so much that he'd pulled the bow across the strings in a terrible, earsplitting screech. No one had wanted to hear him play after that. No one would listen.

Oh, how Baron Von Grump hated monsters. He hated monsters *more* than he hated smiling, talking, breathing, "good mornings," or gum-chewing.

"Laugh now, you pesky monsters," he growled. "You may have won this round, but you have not seen the last of Baron Von Grump!"

"Caw! Caw!" said Edgar.

Baron Von Grump pulled his shutters closed . . . right onto his telescope. The telescope spun around and slapped into his big, bushy, black eyebrows. Baron Von Grump fell back onto the floor with a loud *THUMP*.

"I meant to do that," he said, rubbing his eyebrows.

JUNIOR MONSTER SCOUT
· HANDBOOK ·

The Junior Monster Scout oath:

I promise to be nice, not scary. To help, not harm.

To always try to do my best. I am a monster, but

I am not mean. I am a Junior Monster Scout!

Junior Monster Scout mottos:

By paw or claw, by tooth or wing, Junior Monster Scouts can do anything!

Never say "never" when friends work together!

By tooth or wing, by paw or claw, a Junior Monster Scout does it all!

Junior Monster Scout laws:

Be Kind—A scout treats others the way they want to be treated.

Be Friendly—A scout is open to everyone, no matter how different they are.

Be Helpful—A scout goes out of their way to do good deeds for others . . . without expecting a reward.

Be Careful—A scout thinks about what they say or do *before* they do it.

Be a Good Listener—A scout listens to what others have to say.

Be Brave—A scout does what is right, even if they are afraid, and a scout makes the right decisions . . . even if no one else does.

Be Trustworthy—A scout does what they say they will do, even if it is difficult.

Be Loyal—A scout is a good friend and will always be there for you when you need them.

Junior Monster Scout badges in this book:

Flying Merit Badge

Howling Merit Badge

Teamwork Merit Badge

· ACKNOWLEDGMENTS ·

Much like Doctor Frankenstein, standing before his creation, I want to shout, "It's alive!" For this book and this series are very much alive. But it would not be so without some amazing people who have encouraged, supported, guided, and believed in me along the way. Without them, this book would not be in your hands, and I might just be another mad scientist with an even madder idea.

To my wife, my love, my best friend, Jess—together, we have built the life we always wanted; a life filled with love, writing, and adventure. You inspire me. You challenge me. You encourage and celebrate

87

me, and I know that I have been able to accomplish what I have accomplished so far because of your love and support. I'm glad we're not both vampires, because our mortality makes every moment count. I love you and I am so grateful to have you by my side.

Linda—thanks for your vision and for seeing the potential in these books. I appreciate you challenging me to grow my idea.

Karen—you are a rock star! I am beyond lucky to have such an insightful, supportive, and visionary editor. These books howl at the moon because of you. Thank you for believing in me, for loving my stories, and for taking me under your wing. I cannot wait to see what else we do!

Mom—remember that time we were watching *The Fog*, in Pittsburgh, and you asked me to go outside *in the FOG* and check on the dog? Remember when you and Dad tried to make me go in that crazy haunted Brigantine Castle? Well, thanks, I'm scarred (joking). But seriously, thanks for always feeding me books, for taking me to the library, for encouraging my imagination. It was more important than you'll probably ever realize. Dad, thanks for always working hard to provide for us and for letting me chase dragons . . . even when you didn't understand.

To the late George Romero—thank you for bringing the walking dead into mainstream media culture. And thank you for taking me and Cam to see *Empire Strikes Back* and for dinner. You encouraged a young mind to pursue his passion for storytelling and for monsters.

To the late Gary Gygax—thanks for Dungeons & Dragons. Your game (and a thousand others since) developed a passion for storytelling in me from when I was ten years old and sat, spellbound, listening to local teens battling skeletons in a damp, subterranean tomb.

Kathi Appelt, Sharon Darrow, Tom Birdseye, Amy King, and Lisa John-Clough—you taught me so much about my writing, about the craft, about myself. I will forever be indebted to you.

To my Allies in Wonderland—thank you

for your friendship and for sharing this crazy writing life. We have read, laughed, cried, and created together. We have supported one another. We're all mad here.

To my VCFA family—you are magical people in a magical place. You changed my life. Thank you.

To my SNC family—I love you all. I never thought I could find a place that would fill the hole left by Vermont. I didn't . . . I found something else entirely: a writer's paradise where my heart sings by being around each and every one of you. I am honored and proud to be a part of such an amazing program, inspired by the talented students, and humbled by the masterful faculty. Brian, thank you for making me a part of your magic and for your friendship. Shannon, thank you for making me feel like a needed and integral part of our program.

Eric, I value your friendship so very much and I look forward to writing, creating, and gaming together. Funny when you find a kindred spirit in the middle of life.

Pablo, my brother—thank you for standing by me from the beginning. For your friendship, your love, and always looking out for Jess and me. And hey, thanks for marrying us, Padre Cartaya!

Becca, Josh, Lena, and Maddie—wow, just wow. So much love and thanks for truly being there. For embracing me and loving me and being my family. Thank you. You'll never know how much your kindness has meant. I love you! 10-3 club!

To our amazing children, Zachary, Ainsley, Shane, Logan, Braeden, and Sawyer—I love you all more than you can imagine. Thank you for not grumbling too much when we pulled you to all of those signings and events and book festivals. You've all been so wonderful in this crazy writing life that Jess and I have chosen. I know it has not always been easy, but thank you.

To Donna and Erica—thanks for your insight and great feedback. It's nice to have a smart, supportive, honest, and fun critique group!

To the Frenchtown community—as I write this, we are about a month from the tragic fire that destroyed our home and two beloved businesses. In the midst of this chaos, of losing everything we had (except our lives and computers), you rallied around us and provided everything from kind words and hugs, to clothes and toothbrushes, to food and a place to stay. You supported us. You loved us. You rallied around us and made the nightmare manageable. Without you, I'm not sure I could have finished my revisions on time, let alone functioned like a normal human being. So thank you all, especially you, Caroline. You are a treasured friend and The Book Garden will always be a special place for us. Kandy, the Art Yard, Brad, Ben, Rosella, Carolyn, The United Way,

Peter, Dawn, and a hundred other people I may have neglected to mention but have not forgotten, thank you!

And to my brother, Jack, who would have been in his twenties now. Who laughed hysterically every time I read *Fox in Socks* faster than humanly possible, who taught me to appreciate life—every fleeting, fragile moment of it—I love you. You are not forgotten. You have never been forgotten and I love you, little brother. I miss you.

One final thanks goes out to all of the teachers, librarians, and parents who go out of their way to encourage creativity and foster a love of reading. It was a Young Authors' Day in elementary school, a one-day series of workshops designed to inspire and encourage young creative writers, that had me convinced I wanted to be an author "when I grew up"; that helped me believe that I *could* be an author when "I grew up." Whether or not I actually grew up is up for debate, but I am an author. I did it. And you helped me believe I could. I thank those of you who do the same today for the writers of tomorrow. They need you. We need them.

Crash! Bang! Boo!

CHAPTER
1

"COME ON, FRANKY!" SAID VAMPYRA. "WE'RE missing all the fun!"

"It sounds like a howling good time!" said Wolfy.

"One more bolt to tighten," said Franky. "There! Now my windup monster is all ready for the village's first ever Monster Mash competition!"

The villagers had been so thankful for the Junior Monster Scouts helping them before, that the mayor insisted the Junior Monster Scouts join them for the village's birthday celebration. To show the Junior Monster Scouts that the villagers were no longer afraid of the monsters (it had all been a big misunderstanding), the mayor declared a special contest: a Monster Mash competition. Whoever created the coolest, the craziest, the most wonderful windup monster would win the first place ribbon and a hand-carved cuckoo clock, made by none other than the mayor himself!

Franky set his wrench down and stepped back. His windup mechanical monster hopped up and down, clapping its claws and waving its tentacles.

"That looks great, Franky!" said Wolfy.

"First place ribbon, here I come," said Franky. "That cuckoo clock will look great in my room!"

"Ribbon, schmibbon," said Vampyra. "Party, here I come!"

"I can smell the popcorn from all the way up here!" said Wolfy.

"Smell it all you want," said Franky. "I plan on *tasting* it! Oh, sweet butter, delicious salt . . ."

He closed his eyes and spun in a circle.

"Not if I get there first and eat it all!" teased Vampyra. She flipped her cape around herself and turned into a bat.

Vampyra, Wolfy, and Franky flew, ran, and charged down the road away from Dracula's Castle, hooting, hollering, and howling. They were going to a party tonight, and they were very excited.

Parties are very fun. And birthday parties are even *more* fun. Only, this birthday party was not for just one person. . . . It was for the entire village! The village was one hundred fifty years old today, and they were having a great big birthday party. One hundred fifty is a lot of years, and so there was a lot of celebrating.

Do you know who was *not* celebrating? Do you know who did not like the *pop, pop, POP* of the popcorn machine? Or the bright lights strung from the tents and buildings? Or the marching band? Or the merry-go-round? Or the sugary scent of fresh birthday cake?

That's right . . . Baron Von Grump. He did not like any of those things.

"Caw! Caw!"

And neither did Edgar, his pet crow.

Baron Von Grump folded his arms. He scrunched his big, black, bushy eyebrows. He glared out his window from the top of the rickety Old Windmill.

"Merry-go-round," he muttered. "There's nothing *merry* about it!"

He picked up his violin and set the bow to the strings, but when he tried to play, the popcorn POPPED!

He tried again. *Pop-pop-POP!* Then the music of the merry-go-round spun round and round, right in through his window.

He marched to the other side of the room,

took a deep breath, set the bow to the strings, and . . . *Pop-pop-POP!* Merry-go-round music. *BOOM-BOOM-BOOM* and trumpets trumpeting, horns blaring as the marching band marched through the village.

"Noise, noise, noise, NOISE!" he bellowed.

A long, high-pitched whistling sounded outside his window, and before he could

close the shutters, a single firecracker landed inside his room.

"This is the last—"

POP! BANG! WHIZ!

"Caw!" said Edgar, flapping straight out the window.

"Straw," grumbled Baron Von Grump, collapsing into his chair.

VAMPYRA, WOLFY, AND FRANKY HAD not made it very far when a loud BOOM shook the treetops.

"Was that thunder?" asked Wolfy.

A flash of light lit up the night sky.

"Was that lightning?" asked Vampyra.

A sharp crack and crackle sent jagged sparks across the sky.

"Are those fireworks?" said Franky.

BOOM! FLASH! CRACK! CRACKLE!

"I don't think that's thunder," said Franky.

"Or lightning," Wolfy said.

"Or fireworks," said Vampyra.

Franky, Wolfy, and Vampyra were right. It was *not* thunder, or lightning, or fireworks. And it was *not* coming from the cloudy sky. It was coming from the tallest tower of Castle Dracula, where Franky's grandfather Doctor Frankenstein lived.

A bright green flash of light burst out of the top window of the tower.

"Help!" someone yelled.

"That sounded like my cousin Igor Junior!" said Franky.

"It sounds like he needs our help," said Wolfy.

"If someone is in trouble, better get there on the double!" Vampyra said.

Franky, Wolfy, and Vampyra put their

hands together and said, "Junior Monster Scouts to the rescue! Let's go!"

They turned right back around and raced up the road, back to Castle Dracula and *away* from the party.

• • •

But not everyone heard the cry for help. Not everyone thought something dangerous might be happening. In fact, the villagers thought the bright lights and loud booms and flashes and crackling crackles were a wonderful, spectacular fireworks show.

They oohed. They aahed. They clapped their hands and whistled.

"What a splendid birthday gift for our village!" said the mayor. "Strike up the band! Sound the flügelhorns!" He cleared his throat and fluffed out his magnificent mustache. "Friends, neighbors, villagers one and all, won't you join me in song?"

Hat in hand, the mayor began.

"*Happy birthday to us, happy birthday to us . . .*"

The whole village joined in. You can join in too, but not yet. We'll come back to the birthday song in a moment. Right now, Igor Junior needs some help.

CHAPTER

3

THE JUNIOR MONSTER SCOUTS RAN UP and up and up and up and up and up the stairs. There were a lot of stairs. There were so many stairs that they had to stop halfway to catch their breath.

"How many stairs *are* there!?" said Wolfy. "How tall *is* this tower?"

See? It was a very tall tower with a *lot* of stairs.

"I'm dizzy," said Franky.

And they were spiral stairs. That means
that they went in a circle, up and up and up
and . . . you get the idea.

When they got to the top of the stairs, they found the door to Doctor Frankenstein's laboratory closed. There was a sign on the door. It read:

AWAY ON MAD SCIENTIST BUSINESS.
PLEASE RETURN TOMORROW.

"Nobody is home," said Vampyra.

Wolfy scratched his head. "But we heard—"

"HELP!"

"That is Igor Junior!" said Franky. "And he's inside!"

Franky gripped the doorknob and pulled. The door did not budge. He grabbed it with both hands and pulled harder. It still did not budge. Wolfy wrapped his arms around

Franky, and they both pulled. It budged a teeny bit. Vampyra wrapped her arms around Wolfy, and all three of them pulled. It budged a teeny bit more.

"Igor Junior!" called Franky.

"Franky?" said Igor Junior from the other side of the door.

"Push the door!" Franky said.

He did. He pushed. They pulled. And then . . . the door popped right open, spilling them all into one tangled pile of monsters.

"We heard your cry for help!" said Vampyra.

"And we rushed here to help you!" said Franky.

"Up a lot of steps," Wolfy grumbled.

Igor Junior wrung his hands. "Thank you, Junior Monster Scouts, but I'm in so much trouble! I don't know if you can help. I don't know what to do!"

"What's wrong?" said Franky.

"Yeah," said Vampyra. "What's the problem?"

Igor Junior pointed back into the laboratory. "Look," he said.

Doctor Frankenstein's laboratory was an absolute disaster. Imagine what your room would look like if you pulled out every toy you had and spread them all over the floor. Then you threw your clothes around your room. Then you pulled every sheet, pillow, blanket, and stuffed animal off your bed. Then you tossed everything up in the air and let it lie where it fell. That would be a disaster. But it would *still* not be as bad as what the laboratory looked like.

Tables were turned over. Beakers and vials and jars lay on the floor. Gears ground and groaned. Strange coils hissed and spit sparks. Smoke drifted through the room, and green flashes of light pulsed. A jagged bolt of lightning struck the opening in the ceiling, and crackling arcs of electricity raced down the chains dangling from above.

It was a disaster. A *dangerous* disaster.

"What happened?" said Franky.

Igor Junior buried his face in his hands and moaned.

"Pop and Grandpa told me," Igor Junior said. "They told me and told me and told me."

"What did they tell you?" Vampyra said.

"They said, 'Igor Junior, don't touch that lever.'"

"Let me guess . . . ," said Wolfy.

"Yep," said Igor Junior. "I touched that lever."

BARON VON GRUMP STUFFED COTTON IN his ears. He put on earmuffs. He wrapped a scarf around the earmuffs, but still he could not stop all of that noise, noise, noise, NOISE from getting through.

"Stop oohing," he said. "Stop aahing. Stop blaring those flügelhorns and pounding your drums. And above all . . . STOP. SINGING!"

"Caw, caw!" said Edgar.

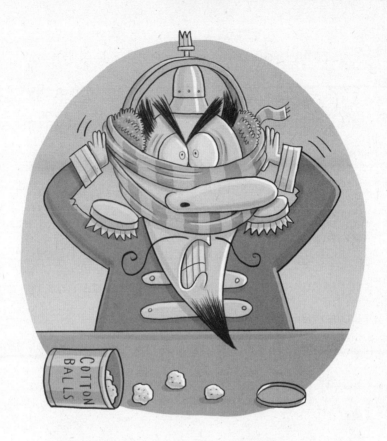

"What did you say?" asked Baron Von Grump. He unwound the scarf. He took off the earmuffs. He unplugged the cotton.

"Caw, caw!" repeated Edgar.

First Baron Von Grump's big, black, bushy

right eyebrow raised. Then his left. Then, ever so slowly, his lips wriggled into a sly and sinister grin. It was the kind of grin someone gets when they are up to no good.

"That is an excellent idea, Edgar," he said.

"Caw, caw!"

Baron Von Grump clapped his hands together and chuckled. He was definitely up to no good.

"Come, my feathered friend," he said to Edgar. "Let us end this celebration once and for all."

Baron Von Grump and Edgar went down the rickety stairs of the rickety windmill. They went through the crooked door and down the winding trail to a small shack. There was a sign on the door. It read:

VILLAGE POWER

DO **NOT** ENTER

THIS MEANS YOU!

Do you think that Baron Von Grump listened?

You're right; he did not. He did not listen at all. He did not listen, he did not follow instructions, and he certainly was not about to behave himself. He marched right past the sign, right through the door, and right into the small room.

Inside the room was a giant machine. It was the size of a refrigerator, with lots of dials and buttons and one big lever. One side of the lever read: ON. The other side read: OFF.

The switch was in the ON position.

Baron Von Grump gripped the lever.

"Caw, caw!" said Edgar.

"Yes, Edgar," said Baron Von Grump. "On three!"

"Caw . . . caw . . . caw!"

Baron Von Grump pulled the lever.

• • •

Do you remember what we were singing a couple of chapters ago? We were singing "Happy Birthday" to the village. Me, you, the mayor, the villagers—we were all singing. There were flügelhorns and the rest of the band. Remember? Okay, good. Let's try this again.

"*Happy birthday to us, happy birthday to us, happy birthday, dear village, happy birthday to—*"

Suddenly the lights went out. The popcorn machine stopped popping. The merry-go-round stopped going round. Everything was dark and quiet and suddenly not-so-merry.

The party had ground to a halt, and I think you know why.

I'm pretty sure you know who was behind it. But the villagers? They did not.

They had no idea why there was no power. Who might have pulled a lever they were not supposed to pull? Who wanted an end to their party celebrations?

But we know who it was. We know *exactly* who it was, and his initials are B. V. G.

CHAPTER
5

FRANKY, WOLFY, VAMPYRA, AND IGOR Junior stood at the open doorway to Doctor Frankenstein's laboratory.

Thunder boomed, lightning crackled, and the whole room was a hissing, spitting, sparking, grinding, flashing mess!

"So all we have to do is pull that lever back to where it was in the first place?" said Franky.

"Yes," said Igor Junior.

"That lever all the way on the other side of the room?" said Wolfy.

"Yes," groaned Igor Junior.

"Then why didn't you just do that in the first place?" Vampyra said.

"Because I was scared," said Igor Junior.

"I don't blame you," Wolfy mumbled.

Franky pulled out his copy of the Junior Monster Scout handbook and opened to the Scout Laws.

"'It may be scary,'" read Franky, "'but a Junior Monster Scout is brave.'"

"'And that means doing what is right,'" said Vampyra, reading over his shoulder.

"'Even if they are afraid,'" finished Wolfy.

"'*Especially* if they are afraid,'" Franky said. "'That's what being brave is.'"

"You'll help me?" said Igor Junior.

"Of course!" said Vampyra.

Igor Junior puffed out his chest. "Then let's go!" he said.

He reached back and took Franky's hand. Franky took Vampyra's hand. Vampyra took Wolfy's hand, and Wolfy . . . Well, I suppose he would have held your hand if you were there with the Junior Monster Scouts, but you were not. So Wolfy did not hold anyone's hand but Vampyra's.

Slowly but surely they crept through the laboratory. Past the hissing steam pipe. Over the sparking wire. Under the grinding gears. Around the spitting cauldron. And right up to the flashing machine with the big red lever.

"Well, this is the one," said Igor Junior.

"That wasn't so bad," said Wolfy.

Thunder boomed overhead, and an arc

of lightning lit up the sky. All four of them jumped. It was loud, and it was scary. But the Junior Monster Scouts and Igor Junior were being brave. Remember? That means doing something even when you are afraid. They were certainly afraid, but they were going to help Igor Junior, and this time Igor Junior wasn't going to *pull* that lever. . . . He was going to *push* it, right back to where it belonged.

"Go ahead," Vampyra said.

"You can do it," said Wolfy.

Igor Junior wiggled his fingers. He squared his shoulders. He took a deep breath. He reached out for the lever—

"Wait!" said Franky. He held up the Junior Monster Scout handbook and said . . .

CHAPTER
6

WE'LL GET BACK TO WHAT FRANKY said. But for now we are going to go to the village, where everything was dark and confusing and no longer fun.

"What's going on?" asked a villager.

"Who turned out the lights?" another villager asked.

"Why did the popcorn stop popping?" asked a third. "How will we have our Monster Mash competition?"

"Oh, man," groaned a fourth villager. "I really wanted that cuckoo clock."

"Everyone stay calm," said the mayor. "I am sure there is a perfectly good explanation for this."

And there *was* an explanation, but the only person it was good for was Baron Von Grump.

Baron Von Grump trudged back to his crooked windmill with an equally crooked grin on his face.

"Caw, caw!" said Edgar.

"Yes," he said, "of course it is dark. We turned off the power. No power, no lights. No lights, no partying."

"Caw, caw?" asked Edgar.

"I'll simply light a candle," said Baron Von Grump. "A nice, soft, soothing candle by which to play my violin. And this time, nothing will get in my way!"

Okay, hold on. You and I know that is probably not true. You and I know that someone is probably going to get in his

way . . . *three* someones . . . and you know who they are: the Junior Monster Scouts!

Which reminds me . . . weren't we waiting to hear what Franky was about to say? We were, weren't we?

Franky quoted the Junior Monster Scout handbook. . . .

"'A SCOUT IS CAREFUL,'" HE SAID. "'They think about what they are going to do *before* they do it.'"

"Do you think it is dangerous?" said Igor Junior.

"It could be," said Vampyra.

"It sure looks dangerous," Wolfy said. "Look at all of those sparks!"

"If it looks dangerous, it probably is dangerous," said Franky.

"But if we don't turn it off, the whole lab will be ruined!" cried Igor Junior. "That lever controls all of the extra electricity for Doctor Frankenstein's experiments!"

"Maybe we don't need to touch the lever," Franky said. "Maybe we can use something else."

"Something with a long reach," said Wolfy.

"And light enough for Igor Junior to hold," said Vampyra.

"Like this broom!" said Igor Junior. He held up a long push broom. "It's light and has a long reach and just might work!"

More lightning flashed. More thunder boomed. More things sparked and hissed and groaned and creaked and popped and flashed.

"You can do it, Igor Junior," said Vampyra.

Igor Junior reached out with the broom. He pressed it against the lever, and then he pushed.

But nothing happened.

He pushed harder.

But still nothing happened.

He pushed as hard as he could, and *still* the lever did not budge.

"It's stuck," he said. "We'll never budge it."

"Maybe we can help," said Franky.

"Never say 'never' when friends work together!" said Wolfy.

Franky, Vampyra, and Wolfy all grabbed the broom with Igor Junior.

"On three!" said Vampyra. "One . . ."

"Two . . . ," said Wolfy.

"Three!" said Franky.

Igor Junior and the Junior Monster Scouts pushed as hard as they could, and finally the lever moved. It clicked right back to where it was before Igor Junior pulled it.

The sparking, groaning, hissing, creaking, and popping all STOPPED. The lightning stopped flashing. The thunder stopped

booming. Doctor Frankenstein's laboratory was back to normal.

Almost. There was still a lot of mess to clean up.

"We did it!" said Vampyra.

"Thank you, Junior Monster Scouts," said Igor Junior. "But look at this mess! I'm going to be in *BIG* trouble."

"You're not the only one in trouble right now," said Wolfy. He pointed out the window, toward the village. "Look!"

BARON VON GRUMP SETTLED BACK INTO his favorite chair. Edgar settled onto his favorite ceiling beam.

It was dark in the windmill. It was dark everywhere, now that the electricity and lights had all gone out. But it was not a spooky dark, not like the Gloomy Woods from the Junior Monster Scouts' last adventure. This dark was like if you were hiding under your favorite blanket and you couldn't really see

anything in detail, just dark, fuzzy shapes.
There was enough moonlight to make sure
you didn't stub your toe or run into a wall.
But otherwise . . . it was pretty dark.

"Now this is more like it," said Baron Von
Grump. "This is just what I need. A nice,
quiet, soothing place to play my music, and
no villagers or Junior Monster Scouts are
going to get in my way!"

"Caw, caw!" said Edgar.

"Yes," said Baron Von Grump, "meddle-
some Junior Monster Scouts always sticking their claws where they don't belong.
But not this time!"

Baron Von Grump shook his fist in the air.
He was still upset about the Junior Monster
Scouts ruining his last plan. If it weren't for

the Scouts, he, Baron Von Grump, would have stopped the villagers' big cheese festival and chased them all away once and for all.

Then he took a deep breath, counted to three, and let it out. This made him feel even more relaxed. It is very important to feel relaxed when you are going to play soothing music. It is also important to stretch before you do activities.

Baron Von Grump stretched his arms out in front of him and spread his fingers wide apart. First he made tiny circles with his thumb. He went in one direction, then the other direction. Then he wiggled both of his pointer fingers, then the middles, then the ring fingers, and finally the pinkies. Then he wiggled them all at the same time.

If you didn't know that Baron Von Grump was stretching his muscles, you might have thought he was casting a spell. But he was not. He was just getting ready to play his violin.

Edgar stretched out his wings and made tiny circles with them. He was not going to play the violin. He was going to clap when Baron Von Grump was finished with his masterpiece song, and he wanted to be ready. He did not want to pull a feather while clapping.

Baron Von Grump unfastened the clasps of his old violin case and opened the lid. A soft ribbon of moonlight covered the polished wood and silvery strings.

Baron Von Grump pulled his violin from

its case. He rested it against his neck and under his chin. He lifted the bow to the strings and took a deep breath. This was the moment he had been waiting for. This was his moment to create his masterpiece, a song that would make him famous. A song that everyone would love! A song that would show everyone just how good he was.

He was about to draw the bow across the strings when he stopped.

"It's too dark," he said.

"Caw?" said Edgar.

"Too dark," said Baron Von Grump. "I cannot see the strings."

"Caw, caw!"

"Yes, I know that I'm the one who made

it dark in the first place," said Baron Von Grump. "That was the idea! But it's a little too dark . . . for me."

"Caw!"

"Another candle!" said Baron Von Grump. "That is an excellent idea!"

Baron Von Grump set his violin down and lit another candle. Now there were two. He placed it upon the open window, next to the first candle, and prepared, once again, to play his violin.

The villagers were not about to sit around and do nothing. They marched right to that power shed . . . and stopped.

The mayor leaned forward and peered at the sign on the door.

"What does it say?" asked a villager.

"It says 'Do not enter,'" said the mayor.

"Does that mean *us*?" asked another villager.

The mayor leaned closer and peered at the sign again.

"It says, 'This means you,'" he said.

"Oh dear," said a third villager. "Now what?"

The mayor held his hat in his hand and turned away from the power shed. "I suppose we'll have to cancel the village birthday party *and* the first ever Monster Mash competition."

9

FRANKY, VAMPYRA, AND IGOR JUNIOR rushed to the window to see what Wolfy was looking at.

"All I see is darkness," said Igor Junior.

"That's just it," said Wolfy. "There's supposed to be a big birthday celebration for the village."

"With popcorn," Franky said. "And the first ever Monster Mash competition that I worked so hard for."

"And a merry-go-round," said Vampyra.

"Let's not forget the merry-go-round."

"That sounds fun," said Igor Junior.

"Exactly," said Wolfy. "But it sure doesn't look like anyone is having fun down there."

"What's everyone looking at?" said a very large rat with a very large belly, munching on a wedge of cheese.

None of the Junior Monster Scouts were surprised to see him. He was the leader of all the rats and lived in the basement of Castle Dracula. He was a very nice rat, even if he had bad manners, like chewing cheese with his mouth open.

"The village," Wolfy said. "There's no birthday celebration."

"It's so dark," said Vampyra.

"Oh yeah," said the rat. He waved his cheese in the air. "The power is out."

Igor Junior peered out the window. "Look!

There's a candle in the Old Windmill!"

"The villagers need light!" said Vampyra. "Electricity!"

"Good thing Doctor Frankenstein has his own power," said Wolfy.

Franky scratched his bolts. He did this when he was thinking really hard. He thought of his mechanical monster for the village's first ever Monster Mash competition. He thought of Doctor Frankenstein's laboratory. He thought of what Wolfy had just said. He thought of the lever that Igor Junior was not supposed to touch but had touched anyway.

"Boris," said Franky. (Boris was the name of the large rat with bad manners.) "Can you gather all the rats and bring them here?"

"What?" asked Boris. "Now? We're having a cheese party!"

"You know what goes great with cheese?" asked Franky.

"More cheese?" Boris asked.

"He has a point," said Wolfy.

"Popcorn," said Franky. "Cheese-covered popcorn."

"Say no more," said Boris. He ran off to gather the rest of the rats.

Wolfy's stomach grumbled and growled. "All this talk of popcorn is making me hungry."

Franky wrapped his arms around his friends. "I've got a plan."

10

BEFORE LONG, BORIS RETURNED WITH the rest of the rats. There were a lot of rats.

"So, what's the plan?" asked Boris.

"Yes," said Igor Junior, "what is the plan?"

Franky smiled. "You know all that sparking, popping, spitting, hissing, crackling electricity?" he said.

"You mean the electricity that almost destroyed the laboratory?" asked Wolfy.

"Yes," said Franky. "It just needed some-where to go!"

"Like the village!" said Vampyra.

Igor Junior did not look happy.

"I'm not so sure, Franky," he said. "That would mean I would have to pull that lever *again*."

"But this time you would be pulling it to help someone," said Vampyra.

"A whole village!" Wolfy said.

"And let's not forget what that means," said Boris the rat. "Cheesy popcorn!"

All the rats cheered. They were very excited about anything that had to do with cheese.

"Well, maybe . . . ," said Igor Junior.

"And this time," said Franky, "you won't pull it alone. We'll all do it."

"You will?" said Igor Junior.

"We sure will," said Wolfy.

Franky told them all his plan. It was a good plan, and soon the rats were running through the night, pulling extension cords down from the castle. The rats ran down the Crooked Trail. They ran past the graveyard, through the Gloomy Woods, and across the covered bridge. They ran right to the village, and when they got there, they did just as Franky had said. They plugged their extension cords into the festival lights, and the merry-go-round, and the popcorn machine. Especially the popcorn machine. Nobody could see the rats because it was so dark. And the rats could stay out of everyone's way because rats are very good at sniffing and hearing in the dark. And when they were done, they ran back the way they had come, straight to Castle Dracula.

They were tired. That was a lot of running. But they knew that all that running meant delicious cheesy popcorn. You would probably run back and forth for delicious cheesy popcorn too.

Boris gave Franky a thumbs-up. He was too out of breath to speak.

"Ready?" said Franky.

"Ready," said Igor Junior. He put his hand on the lever.

Wolfy put his hand on the lever too. Then Vampyra added her hand. And finally Franky added his.

"On three," said Franky.

"One . . . ," said Wolfy.

"Two . . . ," said Vampyra.

"THREE!" said Igor Junior. "Pull that lever!"

Igor Junior and the Junior Monster Scouts pulled the lever. A bolt of lightning flickered in the sky. It hit the lightning rod at the

very top of Castle Dracula. It surged down the laboratory cables. It raced along all the extension cords Boris and the rats had taken to the village.

And then?

A tremendous cheer came from the village!

CHAPTER

11

DO YOU KNOW WHY THE VILLAGERS were cheering? I'm sure you do.

Suddenly the lights were on and the village was all lit up. The merry-go-round was going round and round and up and down. The popcorn machine was pop-pop-popping away. The birthday celebration was right back on! The Monster Mash competition was back on schedule!

"Hip, hip, hooray!" cheered the mayor.

"Hip, hip, hooray!" cheered the villagers.

Go ahead—you try it. Give a big cheer. It feels good, right? Well, now you know how the villagers felt. They were very happy to have their birthday celebration back, even if they didn't know how it had happened.

However, not everyone was happy. . . .

Baron Von Grump had been sitting in his chair. He watched the soft glow of the single candle. He held his violin against his neck and shoulder. He took a deep breath, placed the bow against the strings, and—

WHOOM! The lights of the village shone as bright as day, right in his eyes.

The violin made a horrible screech as

Baron Von Grump fumbled the bow across the strings.

SPLOING! Three of his violin strings broke.

"Caw! Caw!" screeched Edgar.

POP-POP-POP-POP went the popcorn machine.

Baron Von Grump tumbled back out of his chair and landed on the floor with a *THUD.*

"Yeow!" he roared.

"Caw! Caw!" hollered Edgar.

Baron Von Grump jumped to his feet, scrunching his thick, black, angry eyebrows together and waving his hands in the air. "Edgar, what do you mean it's the Junior Monster Scouts?"

"Caw, caw!"

"The power is coming from Castle Dracula?"

"Caw, caw!"

Baron Von Grump pulled at his hair. "Why, you Junior Monster Scouts! Wait until I get my hands on—"

Baron Von Grump tripped over his violin and fell face-first onto the floor with an even louder THUD.

"—youuuu," he moaned.

CHAPTER
12

"WE DID IT!" SAID IGOR JUNIOR.

"You certainly did!" boomed a very loud, very stern voice. "Look at this place!"

"Dad?" said Igor Junior.

Sure enough, Igor Junior's dad, Igor Senior, stood in the laboratory doorway. And just like Baron Von Grump, he did *not* look happy. He was also not alone. Doctor Frankenstein was with him. So were Dracula, Frankenstein, and Wolf

Man. They also did not look happy. No one was looking happy.

It was a very uncomfortable moment.

"Look at my laboratory!" said Doctor Frankenstein.

"What did I say, Igor Junior?" asked Igor Senior. "I said one thing. I said, 'Igor Junior—'"

"'Do *not* pull that lever,'" mumbled Igor Junior.

"And what did you do?" Igor Senior asked.

"I pulled the lever," said Igor Junior.

"And one more question," said Dracula. "What's with all the rats? I thought they lived in the basement."

"We were promised cheesy popcorn," said Boris.

"Yeah," said the rest of the rats.

Now all the adults did not look as angry.
They looked confused. They had no idea
what cheesy popcorn had to do with
anything, let alone the terrible mess in the

laboratory. And they certainly had no idea why the rats would have been promised cheesy popcorn.

"That's the thing," said Vampyra. "Igor Junior did not pull the lever by himself."

"He didn't?" Igor Senior asked.

"Well, maybe the first time," said Franky. "But then we all pulled the lever."

"You did?" asked Frankenstein.

"Why would you do that?" Wolf Man asked. "Why would you pull the lever when you were told not to?"

"To save the village," said Wolfy. "They needed electricity for their birthday cele-bration."

"Don't forget the cheesy popcorn!" said Boris.

"And for their popcorn machines," said Igor Junior.

"And lights so they can judge the windup monsters for the first ever Monster Mash competition," Franky said.

"And for their merry-go-round," said Wolfy.

"We were just trying to help," said Vampyra.

All the adults looked at them for a moment. Nobody said anything. They scrunched their eyebrows. They shuffled their feet. They looked at one another.

"Give us a moment, children," said Dracula.

He and the other parents put their heads together in a huddle. They lowered their voices and talked about adult things in very low, adult tones. Sometimes they pointed. Sometimes they shrugged.

"Thanks for standing by me," said Igor Junior to the Junior Monster Scouts.

Franky clapped him on the shoulder. "That's what friends do."

Finally the adults turned back around.

Dracula cleared his throat. "Okay, kids," he said. "Because you were honest and did what you were *not* supposed to do for a good and helpful reason, you are not grounded. You may go to the village birthday celebration *after* you have helped Igor Junior clean up this mess of a laboratory."

"Every bolt, beaker, and bucket of parts," said Doctor Frankenstein.

"And you, Igor Junior," said Igor Senior. "Because you pulled the lever the first time, when you were specifically told *not* to, you are grounded . . ."

Igor Junior's lip trembled. He just nodded and stared at the floor.

"After you enjoy the village birthday celebration and a bucket of cheesy popcorn," finished Igor Senior.

Igor Junior looked up with a surprised smile on his face. "Really?" he said.

"A big birthday bash like this does not happen every day, and you did help make it possible," said Igor Senior. "But starting tomorrow, you'll be doing double chores for a week!"

Igor Junior's lip was no longer trembling.

"Thanks, Pop. And I'm sorry. I'll make sure to listen from now on."

"Well, what are you waiting for?" said Wolf Man. "The quicker you clean, the quicker you get to that party."

"And the cheesy popcorn," said Boris.

Franky, Wolfy, Vampyra, and Igor Junior all put their hands together.

"'Teamwork' on three," Franky said.

"One . . . two . . . three . . . TEAMWORK!" they all shouted.

Igor Junior and the Junior Monster Scouts sprang into action to clean up Doctor Frankenstein's laboratory. Even Boris and the rats helped.

13

IT DID NOT TAKE LONG FOR IGOR JUNIOR and the Junior Monster Scouts to clean up the laboratory. Things go much quicker when everyone lends a hand. Soon the laboratory was just as Doctor Frankenstein and Igor Senior had left it.

"Okay," said Wolf Man, "it looks like you monsters earned your trip to the birthday celebration."

"And the first ever Monster Mash

competition," said Frankenstein. He winked at Franky.

"And that cheesy popcorn," said Igor Senior.

Boris and the rats cheered.

"But be back before sunrise!" said Dracula. He looked at Vampyra. "You know what the sun does to your complexion."

The Junior Monster Scouts, Igor Junior, and the swarm of rats did not waste any time leaving the castle and heading straight for the village.

Peter the piper, their friend from the village, was the first to see them.

"Hello, Junior Monster Scouts!" he said. "I was hoping you would come to the party. I made a very cool monster for the competition!"

"Hi, Peter!" said Vampyra. "This is our friend Igor Junior. And you know the rats. . . ."

Peter did indeed know the rats. He had helped the Junior Monster Scouts lead them out of the village during their last adventure.

"We're only here for some popcorn," said Boris. "Then it's back to the castle for us."

"Come on," said Peter to the rats. "A big bucket of cheesy popcorn, coming right up. Nice to meet you, Igor Junior. You should check out the merry-go-round. It is a lot of fun!"

Igor Junior and the Junior Monster Scouts took his advice. They went round and round and round and up and down and up and down.

"I think I'm getting dizzy," said Wolfy.

"Welcome to the party, Junior Monster Scouts!" said the mayor. "Do we have you to thank for turning on the lights? We almost had to cancel our party . . . *and* the very special, first ever Monster Mash competition!"

"You are very welcome," Vampyra said. "It was Franky's idea."

"Only because Igor Junior pulled the lever and created all that electricity," said Franky.

"Out-of-control electricity," muttered Igor Junior.

"Is that what that was?" asked the mayor. "We thought it was fireworks."

The mayor and the Junior Monster Scouts laughed.

"Let's not forget the rats," Wolfy said. "They helped too!"

"Of course!" said the mayor. "How about joining us in one big round of 'Happy Birthday'?"

The villagers gathered around. The band

marched in with their drums and horns and clanging cymbals. The mayor raised his bullhorn to his lips, and everyone— including the Junior Monster Scouts, Igor Junior, and Boris and the rats—sang.

"*Happy birthday to us, happy birthday to us,*

happy birthday to our village . . . Happy birth-day to us!"

It was a wonderful, loud, cheer-filled song. It made everyone happy. Well, almost everyone. There was one person who was *not* happy. You know who he is, and we'll come back to him in a moment. But for now, let's sit back and enjoy the big smiles and good cheer of the villagers, the Junior Monster Scouts, and the cheesy popcorn–stuffed rats.

I'll bet you want some cheesy popcorn now, don't you?

Me too. All this talk of cheese and pop-corn has me hungry.

Where was I? Oh, yes . . . the birthday cele-bration. Igor Junior and the Junior Monster

Scouts played games, sang songs, and rode the merry-go-round at least a dozen times. At the end of the party, everyone gathered for the big Monster Mash competition. There were many cool, crazy, wonderful windup monsters. The mayor had a very difficult time choosing. But in the end, the coolest, craziest, most wonderful windup monster belonged to . . . Franky Stein! The mayor hung the first place ribbon around his neck and awarded him his very own, hand-carved cuckoo clock. Peter the piper came in second.

The Junior Monster Scouts had a grand time, and before long it was time to go home. After all, they had promised to be home before sunrise, and a Junior Monster

Scout *always* keeps a promise.

They shook hands, waved good-bye, and promised to visit again soon. They even got balloons before they left. Balloons make everything better, don't you think? And when they got back to the castle, the Junior Monster Scouts promised to visit Igor Junior *after* he was done being grounded.

"Thanks for saving the day, Junior Monster Scouts," said Igor Junior.

"Sure thing. But remember . . . ," said Vampyra.

"What's that?" Igor Junior said.

"Don't pull that lever!" said Vampyra, Franky, and Wolfy at the same time.

Igor Junior and the Junior Monster Scouts all laughed.

"OKAY, JUNIOR MONSTER SCOUTS," SAID Frankenstein. "Time for tonight's scout meeting. We have a little time before the sun is up."

Franky, Wolfy, and Vampyra gathered around the table in the castle dungeon. It was a big table in the middle of a very big dungeon. Dracula and the Wolf Man sat down too.

"I know you were only helping," said

Frankenstein, "but that was a very danger-ous laboratory. You could have been hurt!"

"We were very careful," said Vampyra.

"Yeah, we used a broom to touch the lever instead of our hands," said Wolfy.

"That was good thinking," said Wolf Man. "Which is why we think you three earned your Safety Merit Badges."

"For being smart in how you handled a dangerous situation," said Dracula.

Franky, Wolfy, and Vampyra smiled.

"You also earned your Loyalty Merit Badge," said Dracula.

"For sticking by Igor Junior and not letting him take all the blame," Frankenstein said.

"And helping him clean up his mess," said Wolf Man.

Franky, Vampyra, and Wolfy all high-fived.

"Okay, scouts," said Wolf Man. "Line up."

Franky, Vampyra, and Wolfy lined up, proudly wearing their Junior Monster Scout sashes. Wolf Man stopped before each of them and pinned on their Safety Merit

Badges. Dracula stopped before each of them and pinned on their Loyalty Merit Badges.

Then Frankenstein cleared his throat. "Ahem," he said. "We have one more badge to present."

"You do?" said Franky.

"I heard that the mayor gave you a first-place ribbon," said Frankenstein.

"And a very fine, hand-carved cuckoo clock," said Dracula.

"Franky won those in the first ever Monster Mash competition!" said Wolfy.

"He made the coolest, craziest, most wonderful windup monster!" Vampyra said.

Frankenstein arched one eyebrow and winked at Franky. "Why don't we wind it up and see how it does?"

Franky gave the winding key one, two, three, four, five big turns and let go. His mechanical monster hopped up and down and back and forth, clapping its claws and waving its tentacles while the music box inside played a haunted tune.

Franky, Wolfy, and Vampyra danced along with it.

"Great job, Franky," said Dracula. "You earned your Gadget Merit Badge for your creation."

Frankenstein pinned the badge on Franky's sash and patted his shoulder. "Good job, Franky. Good job, all three of you!"

"You know what time it is!" said Wolf Man. He leaped up on the table and howled.

"Time to say the Scout oath!" said Dracula. "And get to bed before the sun rises."

Franky, Vampyra, and Wolfy all held hands and said, "I promise to be nice, not scary. To help, not harm. To always try to do my best. I am a monster, but I am not mean. I am a Junior Monster *Scout*!"

And so this particular tale comes to an end.

Almost . . .

CHAPTER

15

BARON VON GRUMP TRUDGED BACK TO
the small shack at the edge of the village,
the one with the sign on the door that read:

VILLAGE POWER
DO NOT ENTER
THIS MEANS YOU!

"Bah," he said. "I'll bet it was those meddling monsters and their junior scout
goodness that ruined my plan."

189

He opened the door and went in, even though the sign said NOT to enter . . . again.

"Caw, caw!" Edgar said.

"I know what it says!" growled Baron Von Grump. He marched over to the big tall machine with dials and buttons and one big lever.

"Everyone has electricity now but me!" he said. "Me! Baron Von Grump! If those annoying villagers have electricity, then *I* want electricity."

He traced his crooked finger along the row of buttons until he found the one labeled:

WINDMILL

He pushed the button. "One last step," he said, grasping the lever.

There was a sign hanging on the lever. The sign read: DO **NOT** PULL THIS LEVER!

"Caw, caw!" said Edgar. He flew in circles around Baron Von Grump.

"I am aware of what it says," sneered Baron Von Grump. "Nobody tells Baron Von Grump what to do!"

"Caw!" Edgar said. He flew in circles around the little shack.

"Coward!" yelled Baron Von Grump.

He wrapped his other hand around the lever and—

You know . . . this sounds oddly familiar, doesn't it? What was Igor Junior told? Do you remember? Perhaps we should give Baron Von Grump one final warning. Ready? Okay, one . . . two . . . three:

Baron Von Grump, do NOT pull that lever!

Of course, he did not listen.

"Edgar?" he groaned. "Could you, perhaps . . . *spring* me free?"

JUNIOR MONSTER SCOUT
· HANDBOOK ·

The Junior Monster Scout oath:

I promise to be nice, not scary. To help, not harm.

To always try to do my best. I am a monster, but

I am not mean. I am a Junior Monster Scout!

Junior Monster Scout mottos:

By paw or claw, by tooth or wing, Junior Monster Scouts can do anything!

Never say "never" when friends work together!

By tooth or wing, by paw or claw, a Junior Monster Scout does it all!

Junior Monster Scout laws:

Be Kind—A scout treats others the way they want to be treated.

Be Friendly—A scout is open to everyone, no matter how different they are.

Be Helpful—A scout goes out of their way to do good deeds for others . . . without expecting a reward.

Be Careful—A scout thinks about what they say or do *before* they do it.

Be a Good Listener—A scout listens to what others have to say.

Be Brave—A scout does what is right, even if they are afraid, and a scout makes the right decisions . . . even if no one else does.

Be Trustworthy—A scout does what they say they will do, even if it is difficult.

Be Loyal—A scout is a good friend and will always be there for you when you need them.

Junior Monster Scout badges in this book:

Gadget Merit Badge

Loyalty Merit Badge

Safety Merit Badge

· ACKNOWLEDGMENTS ·

Having rambled through pages of acknowledgments in book 1, *The Monster Squad*, I am going to keep this much shorter.

As always, I am so grateful for the love, support, and encouragement from my wife, best friend, and adventuring partner, Jessica. She not only champions me and my work, but also challenges me and inspires me. Thank you, love! I'm so happy to be on this writing journey together.

Mad respect and admiration for my superstar editor, Karen Nagel, and the entire Aladdin team. I know you love these books as much as I do, and you've really made my vision become something even greater than I anticipated. Thank you!

Thank you, Linda Epstein, for your hard work and dedication to the project. You saw it was more than my initial idea and encouraged me to make something more of it. I really appreciate that.

Many thanks to the amazingly talented Ethan Long for his fun, zany, adorable illustrations. Wow! I just want to hug those Junior Monsters!

I want to thank our children, Zachary, Ainsley, Shane, Logan, Braeden, and Sawyer not only for their excitement and pride in our books, but for all of the sacrifices they've had to make and adjustments they've been through. Thank you.

Thank YOU, the readers . . . because

without you, there'd be no book. Or maybe there'd be a book, but no reader. And what good is a good story without a reader? If a tree falls in the forest, and nobody is around to hear it, does it still make a noise? How much wood could a woodchuck chuck if a woodchuck could chuck wood? Anyway, thanks for reading my book!

Finally, a great big thank you to all of the librarians (media specialists), teachers, and parents who battle digital distractions every day and fight to put books in the hands of young readers. Your commitment to reading, imagination, and creativity is SO important. Thank you!

Oh, and thank you, coffee.

It's Raining Bats and Frogs!

FOR JACK

★ ★ ★ ★

I wish you were here
to read it.

CHAPTER

1

"ON YOUR MARK," SAID FRANKY.

"Get set," said Vampyra.

"Float!" Wolfy said.

Franky, Vampyra, and Wolfy set their paper boats in the river and watched them sail away. It was springtime, and the April showers had made a wet, muddy mess of everything. Yesterday, the Junior Monster Scouts had raced frogs across the lily pads in the swamp. Today, they were racing boats in the river.

"Look at them go!" said Franky.

"I'll bet they go all the way to the water-fall," Wolfy said. "I wonder whose boat will win the race."

Franky and Wolfy ran along the river-bank, following the boats. Vampyra spun three times in a circle and POOF, turned into a bat. She flittered ahead of them, flapping her bat wings. She was practicing for her Flying Merit Badge.

"Come on, slowpokes," she said. "What's taking you so long?"

"No fair!" Wolfy said. "You can fly."

"And you don't have to run through this mud," said Franky. "It's slowing me down!"

"Excuses, excuses," Vampyra teased.

Wolfy dropped to all fours and raced

ahead of Franky. "Race you to the water-fall, Vampyra!"

"You're on," she said.

"Guys?" said Franky. But Wolfy and Vampyra pulled ahead of Franky and even ahead of the boats. "You go ahead," he said. "I'll just keep an eye on the boats."

The boats, however, did not need much keeping an eye on. They bobbed and swirled and raced along the river while Franky did his best to keep up.

The Junior Monster Scouts were not the only ones enjoying the light rain. The villagers were also celebrating spring. No afternoon showers were going to keep *them* inside. They put on their raincoats, rain hats, and rain boots, and they jumped from puddle to puddle with resounding *kersplashes*! They stomped and splashed and sang in the rain.

"Attention, villagers!" said the mayor. "I declare an umbrella contest!" He wiped the rain from his mustache. "Prize goes to the best decorated umbrella!"

"There should be a parade!" said Peter, the young piper.

"Quack, quack!" said the ducks, paddling about in a deep puddle.

And just in case you don't speak duck, "quack, quack" means *Yes, we should have a rainy day parade and an umbrella contest, and we will be the judges.*

"Oh, this will be splendiferous!" said the mayor.

* * *

But not everybody was enjoying the rain. Not everybody was excited about umbrellas and puddles and parades.

"Caw, caw!" said Edgar, Baron Von Grump's friend and pet crow.

"Yes," said the baron, "of course I—"

PLINK!

A big, wet drop of water fell from the ceiling and landed directly on the tip of his nose.

"Don't you think I know that we need another—"

PLINK! PLUNK!!

Two big, wet drops of water dripped from the leaky ceiling of the crooked old windmill and fell right atop Baron Von Grump's head.

"—bucket," growled Baron Von Grump.

"Caw, caw!" said Edgar.

"Well, don't just sit there. Grab an empty—"

PLINK! PLUNK! PLINK!!

Three big, wet drops of water dripped from the ceiling in three different spots.

"—pail," said Baron Von Grump.

He moved one bucket. *PLINK*. He adjusted a pail. *PLUNK*. He slid a can over to catch another drop. *PLINK*. He set one of his boots under a fourth drop. *PLUNK*.

Edgar hopped from beam to beam, pointing at new leaks and new drops.

"Caw, caw!" he crowed.

"Oh, confound it!" said Baron Von Grump. "Rain, rain, go away, come again . . . NEVER!"

PLINK, PLUNK, PLINK, PLUNK, PLINK, PLUNK . . .

Baron Von Grump glared at his leaky ceiling.

PLINK!

And caught a raindrop right in his eye.

CHAPTER

2

VAMPYRA FLIPPED AND FLITTERED AND fluttered along the riverbank. She was ahead of Wolfy. She was far ahead of their paper boats. And she was *very* far ahead of Franky. She was sure she was going to earn her Flying Merit Badge . . . as long as she could keep her wings going long enough. But right now, she needed a rest.

"Whew, flying sure is tiring," she said.

"So is swimming," someone croaked from the edge of the river.

"Laguna!" said Vampyra. She landed and changed back into a vampire.

Laguna lived in the swamp with her mom, dad, and sixteen younger swamplings. But

today, she was not in the swamp. She was in the river.

Laguna pulled herself onto the river-bank and sprawled out in the wet grass. She stretched her webbed toes and spread her webbed fingers. Her gills heaved in and out. She seemed very tired. Even more tired than Vampyra.

"What are you doing in the river, Laguna?" Vampyra asked.

"Swimming lessons," Laguna groaned.

Wolfy and Franky finally caught up with them. They were out of breath too.

"I think I'm going to hurl a hair ball," Wolfy said.

"I think I swallowed a fish," said Laguna.

Laguna's mom popped up above the

surface of the river. She swam in circles on her back. She was an excellent swimmer.

"Hello, kids," she said.

"Hi, Mrs. Lagoon," they all answered.

"Laguna is going to take her swimming test today," said Mrs. Lagoon. "But first, she has a bit of practice to do."

"Mommmmm," said Laguna. "I can't swim to the other side."

"Sure you can," said Mrs. Lagoon. "It just takes practice, and for you to believe in yourself."

"You can totally do it," Vampyra said.

"I have a great idea," said Mrs. Lagoon. "Maybe Vampyra, Franky, and Wolfy will take lessons with you!"

"No way!" said Wolfy. "My fur will be a stinky, wet mess."

Franky shuffled his feet. "Um . . . my bolts might get rusted."

"I'd rather fly," Vampyra said with a grin.

"See, Mom?" said Laguna. "Even the Junior Monster Scouts are scared of swimming."

"Well, I wouldn't say we are *scared*," mumbled Wolfy.

"I would," said Franky.

Mrs. Lagoon floated on her back and blew a long jet of water up into the air. "There is nothing to be scared of," she said. "Besides . . . isn't swimming one of the Junior Monster Scout merit badges?"

Franky flipped through his scout hand-book. Sure enough, swimming *was* a Junior Monster Scout merit badge.

"Come on, kids," said Mrs. Lagoon. "I'll help you all learn how to swim. You'll get your merit badges, and Laguna won't feel so scared with her friends alongside her."

Laguna sat up and clapped her webbed fingers. "Oh, will you?" she asked. "Will you? Will you? Will you? Puhleeaaazzze!"

Wolfy looked at Vampyra. Vampyra looked at Franky. Franky stared at his scout hand-book.

"I suppose?" he said nervously.

Meanwhile, back in the village, the umbrella contest was well underway. There were bright umbrellas and striped umbrellas, umbrellas with swirls and spirals and flowers and polka dots. Tall umbrellas and short umbrellas, round umbrellas and square umbrellas.

"Oh, this is absolutely splendiferous!" said the mayor. "Truly wonderific! Everyone, get in line. The parade is about to begin!"

"Quack, quack, quack!" said the ducks.

They were very excited for the parade and even more excited to help judge the umbrella contest.

"Yes, yes, of course," the mayor said to the ducks. "You can join our parade as well!"

The ducks fluffed their feathers and waddled into line.

"Quack, quack, quack!"

(That means *Thank you* and *We are very pleased to accept your invitation.* As you can see, these were very polite ducks.)

"Okay, Peter," said the mayor. "Lead the way!"

Peter picked up his flute and led the parade through the town. Rain boots squelched and splashed in puddles. Ducks quacked. And everyone—*everyone*—was singing in the rain.

Everyone but Baron Von Grump in his crooked, leaky windmill, that is. *He* was NOT singing.

And if you know anything about Baron Von Grump, you will know that he was not singing because he was *not* happy.

And if he was not happy, sooner or later (probably sooner) he was going to form a plan. A sinister, diabolical plan to make him happy . . . and everyone else *unhappy*.

MRS. LAGOON WAITED UNTIL THE JUNIOR Monster Scouts had changed into their bathing suits before continuing Laguna's swimming lessons. The rain was light and warm and kind of refreshing. It was like being squirted with a hundred little squirt guns filled with warm water. Except not in your eye, because nobody likes that.

Laguna waded out into the water until she was up to her waist. Franky, Wolfy, and

Vampyra stood at the edge of the river.

"Come on, guys," said Laguna. "The water feels nice."

Wolfy dipped his toe in. "Feels nice from right here," he said.

"Do any of you know how to swim?" asked Mrs. Lagoon.

"I can doggy paddle," said Wolfy.

"I can float," said Franky.

"I prefer to keep my wings dry," Vampyra said, turning into a bat and then back into herself.

"Laguna," said Mrs. Lagoon, "why don't you show the Junior Monster Scouts what you've learned so far?"

Laguna smiled. She had an audience now. Sometimes it's fun to do things when you have an audience. Sometimes they clap and cheer and say things like "Wow!" and "Way to go!" and "I wish I could do that!" That is exactly what happened with Laguna. While she swam back and forth, kicking her legs and moving her arms, Franky, Wolfy, and Vampyra were saying those very same things.

When she was finished, they clapped and cheered some more.

"You sure are a good swimmer," said Franky.

"Thanks," said Laguna. "But I still don't know if I'm ready to go out *there*." She pointed to the middle of the river. "I can touch the ground here. I can't touch there."

Mrs. Lagoon said, "If you can swim here,

then you can swim there. It just takes courage. And I'll be right there with you to help
you if you get tired."

Laguna still did not seem convinced. It
can be very scary to do something when
you haven't done it before.

"I'd feel a lot better if the Junior Monster
Scouts were swimming too," said Laguna.

She looked at Franky. Franky looked at
Wolfy. Wolfy looked at Vampyra. Vampyra
looked at her feet.

"Okay," said Wolfy, taking one full step
into the water. "I can't believe I'm doing
this, but . . . I'll take swimming lessons too."

"You will?" asked Laguna.

Franky gulped and stepped into the
water. "Me too."

"Oh, yay!" said Laguna.

Vampyra sighed and stepped in next to them. "Ah, what the heck," she said.

"Oh, you brave Junior Monster Scouts!" said Mrs. Lagoon. "We'll have you swimming in no time. Now, the first step is . . ."

Mrs. Lagoon and Laguna began the Junior Monster Scouts' swimming lessons.

Baron Von Grump marched back and forth across the creaky floor of his leaky windmill. He placed a bucket here. He placed a bucket there. And with every new bucket, with every *plink* and *plunk* and *plink-plunk* of water, he grew even more grumpy than he already was. Edgar hopped from one leak to another, stuffing straw into holes. But every time he plugged one hole, another one sprang a leak.

"Caw, caw!" said Edgar.

"Of course it keeps leaking!" growled Baron Von Grump. "It won't stop leaking until the

rain goes away. This old windmill—"

Baron Von Grump stopped talking. He stopped marching. He stopped placing buckets and pails. One side of his lip turned up, then the other, and suddenly he had the most sinister grin on his grumpy face.

"Caw?" asked Edgar.

"Yes, Edgar, I have an idea . . . a plan . . . a solution to get rid of this rain and splashing and singing and quacking."

See? What did I tell you? It was only a matter of time before Baron Von Grump had a plan. He was not at all fond of this frolicking nonsense. In fact, he did not like *any* celebration. He hadn't liked the village's cheese festival, or their 150th birthday party, and he was not about to start liking this springtime rain celebration.

Who celebrates rain? he thought. They should be indoors, staying dry and *quiet.* Quiet . . . What he wouldn't do for some peace and quiet.

Baron Von Grump slowly lifted his head up to the ceiling and stared past the beams, through a hole in the roof, to the giant wooden paddles of the old windmill . . .

PLINK!

. . . and caught a big old raindrop right in his eye.

CHAPTER
4

LET US GO BACK TO THE VILLAGE.

It was a grand sight to behold. Peter led a long line of villagers and ducks through the streets. They sang. They splashed in every puddle with their galoshes. ("Galoshes" is a fun and fancy word for rain boots. Try saying it. It's fun, right? Galoshes.) They twirled their umbrellas. The mayor wore his finest raincoat and his brightest rain hat and stood at the grandstand with several of the ducks, clapping and cheering for every umbrella that passed by. The mayor and the ducks had to judge the best umbrella, and it was very difficult because there were so many wonderful umbrellas of every shape, size, and color.

A small gust of wind picked up. It blew the mayor's brightest rain hat right off his head.

One very thoughtful duck tried to fly over and pick up the mayor's hat, but an even stronger gust of wind flipped the poor duck this way and that. She landed in a puddle with a quack and a splash.

"Oh dear!" said the mayor. "Hold on to your—"

The mayor was going to say "umbrellas."

He was going to tell everyone to hold on to their umbrellas, but before he could say "umbrellas," a superstrong gale of wind howled through the village and pulled umbrellas right out of villagers' hands. It flipped umbrellas inside out. Why, it even lifted one surprised villager right off her feet and would have carried her away if she had not quickly let go of her polka-dot umbrella!

It got windier.

And windier.

And so windy that it

almost blew these words off the page.

"It's working!" said Baron Von Grump. "Flap harder, Edgar!"

Edgar would have replied if he could have. He would have said, "Caw, caw!" which would have meant "How much longer do I have to keep flying in circles?" But he could not reply. He had a string held tightly in his beak. That string was attached to a crank. That crank was attached to the giant wooden paddles of the old windmill. The harder he flapped, the harder he flew. The harder he flew, the faster the crank spun. The faster the crank spun, the faster the windmill paddles turned. And the faster the windmill paddles turned, the stronger the gusts of wind howled through the village, blowing hats off heads and umbrellas out of hands.

However, hats and umbrellas were *not*

what Baron Von Grump was trying to blow away. The rain clouds were. Each little spring rain cloud was being blown out of the village, pushed farther and farther away, until they were swept out entirely. They were pushed right out past the covered bridge, over the Gloomy Woods, and then, once they were far enough from the windmill, drifted toward the lake on their own.

With no clouds, there was no rain. With no rain, there was no reason for raincoats and umbrellas and certainly not for galoshes. The parade was over, the umbrella contest was canceled, and the villagers had no choice but to retreat to their homes. It was far too windy to stay outside without holding on very tight to something so that you did not blow away. The ducks couldn't even fly in this wind, and that made them very sad.

"Quack," said a very sad duck. That means *I wish it weren't so windy*, in case you don't speak duck.

Baron Von Grump listened. There was no plinking. There was no plunking. He slowly raised his eyes to the leaky windmill ceiling, but the leaks were gone. No drips or drops fell into his eye!

"Just a bit more, Edgar!" he said. "Let's make sure those rain clouds are pushed far and away for good."

Edgar flew harder and the crank spun faster. The paddles whipped around in a circle like a giant fan, blowing everything away from the old windmill and the

village. But poor Edgar was getting tired. Very tired. He was doing all the work. He was having a hard time keeping up with the windmill blades and the crank, since they were spinning so fast. On top of that, he was getting dizzy!

Edgar opened his beak for a very tired, very dizzy "Cawwwww . . ."

And the rope he was holding flew out of his mouth. The windmill paddles kept spinning faster and faster, and Edgar couldn't stop them. He couldn't slow them down. Every single cloud was pushed away from the old windmill and the village, drifting out over the lake, where they began to form one . . . big . . . GIANT cloud!

CHAPTER 5

LAGUNA AND MRS. LAGOON SHOWED THE Junior Monster Scouts four swimming steps:

- Float.
- Kick.
- Crawl.
- Turn your head side to side.

"It's very important that you do not panic," said Mrs. Lagoon. "If you feel tired, or scared, just tread water. You already know how to do that. Just keep those feet moving like you're pedaling a bicycle and use your hands to spread little circles across the water."

"Like this?" said Franky. He waded in a little deeper and did just as Mrs. Lagoon had instructed.

"Just like that!" said Mrs. Lagoon.

"Show-off," said Vampyra. She splashed Franky and Wolfy.

"Look, Mom," said Laguna, "the rain is gone and the sun is out!"

"The clouds are all over the lake now," said Wolfy.

It was true. All the rain clouds had moved over the lake and were starting to clump together, one by one.

"Well, it looks like a perfect afternoon for swimming lessons," said Mrs. Lagoon.

"And my swimming test!" said Laguna. She was feeling much braver with the Junior Monster Scouts in the water with her.

"I can't wait to see you swim out to that marker!" said Vampyra. "You'll pass your swim test in no time."

"I'll bet you'll all be able to pass that test before you know it," said Mrs. Lagoon. "Now let's get swimming. Laguna will help me show you each of the steps. Ready?"

"Ready!" said Franky.

"Ready," said Wolfy.

"Ready?" said Vampyra. She was not so sure.

But whether they were really ready

(like Franky), or kind of ready (like Wolfy), or somewhat, but not really, ready (like Vampyra), they all followed Laguna and Mrs. Lagoon a little bit farther out into the water.

First it was up to their knees. Then up to their waists. Then right up under their chins.

"Let's practice those strokes," said Mrs. Lagoon. "Make your body as light as you can, and float on the surface. Kick your legs, use your arms and hands to crawl through the water, and turn your head from side to side."

"Wow," said Laguna. "You Junior Monster Scouts sure are quick learners!"

It was true. Franky, Wolfy, and Vampyra were swimming back and forth while Laguna and Mrs. Lagoon cheered and clapped and said things like "Good job!" and "Way to kick those legs!"

They were having a wonderful time. A spectacular time! Splashing and swimming and laughing. The sun was shining and the birds were . . . not singing. That was odd. No birds were singing or chirping. No bunny rabbits were hopping along the bank of the river. It was a bit unusual.

But they did not notice. They were too busy having fun.

"Ready for your test, Laguna?" asked Mrs. Lagoon.

"I sure am," Laguna said.

"All you have to do is swim out to that floating marker and then swim back," said Mrs. Lagoon. "I'll be close by in case you need help." Mrs. Lagoon turned to the Junior Monster Scouts and said, "It's important to remember that you should never swim alone."

Laguna took a deep breath. She stretched her arms. She stretched her legs. Then she pushed forward and began her swim out to the floating marker.

"Way to float, Laguna!" said Mrs. Lagoon.

"Look at her kick!" said Wolfy.

"Look at her crawl with those strokes," said Franky.

"Look at her move her head from side to side to breathe," Vampyra said.

It was true—Laguna was doing a fine job and would be at that floating marker in no time. But those clouds over the lake? They were getting bigger and darker.

To be honest, those clouds are making me a bit nervous for Laguna and the Junior Monster Scouts. Gulp.

CHAPTER

6

THE RIVER WAS NOT THE ONLY PLACE the sun was shining. It was shining over the village, but the villagers could not enjoy it because the winds from the old windmill were so strong that anything not nailed down was whisked up, up, and away.

It's true!

An apple cart, a wagon filled with hay, even an old lady knitting in her rocking chair all flew up, up, and away. (Don't

247

worry—the old lady knitting was saved at the last minute. One quick-thinking villager caught the end of her yarn and pulled her back to safety.)

The villagers had to bring all their cows, horses, goats, chickens, sheep, and pigs into their houses so that the animals did not blow away. And don't forget the ducks! The ducks had to squeeze in as well. And the village cats, and the village dogs. It was very crowded. It was also very loud. It sounded something like this:

"I QUACK sure MOO hope BAAA the WOOF wind MEOW stops OINK soon NEIGHHH COCK-A-DOODLE-DOO!"

But do you know where it was not crowded? And not windy? And not rainy?

Where the sun was also shining? That's right—in the creaky, crooked old windmill where Baron Von Grump lived.

Perhaps, dear reader, you are saying, "Here we go again. . . . Baron Von Grump has set his plan in motion. He's such a grump! And the village needs to be saved *again*. When will the villagers ever learn? And the Junior Monster Scouts will need to save the day." And you would be right! Of course the Junior Monster Scouts will have to save the villagers, but how? Isn't it exciting? Here we go again! Now back to our story . . .

Baron Von Grump stood at the wide-open window and looked out over the village. He drew a deep breath, first with his right nostril, and then with his left, and then, finally, with both of his nostrils.

"What a glorious spring day," he said. He scrunched his eyebrows together and glared at the village. "At last."

Edgar flew in a crooked line right to the corner of the room and collapsed. He was still very, *very* dizzy.

"Perhaps some music will make you feel better, eh?" said Baron Von Grump.

"Cawwww?" Edgar said.

"Yes, something zesty," said Baron Von Grump.

"Caw . . ."

"And lively."

"Caw!"

"Yes, yes! Something you can dance to!"

Baron Von Grump marched straight to the cabinet where he kept his sheet music.

"I've got just the thing," he said. He riffled through his music and held up one page filled with musical notes. "This? No!" He held up another. "How about—no!" He scanned a third. "Too slow." He pushed his face against a fourth. "Rubbish!" He looked at a fifth and a sixth and a seventh and said, "Too soft . . . too loud . . . too weird."

Then Baron Von Grump's eyes settled on something. Something that was sitting right there, in front of his face, the whole time. There, atop the cabinet where he kept his sheet music, sat a small, framed picture of a small boy holding a very small violin. That small boy had very big, bushy, black

eyebrows. It was none other than little Baron Von Grump. He did not look grumpy in the picture. He looked quite happy. He looked like someone had just given him a balloon, and, a puppy, and a piece of cake with two scoops of ice cream and said,

"Here, have this whole pitcher of fizzy soda all to yourself."

Baron Von Grump set down all his sheet music and held the small picture. His eyebrows lifted and his lips did a weird thing that they rarely did: they smiled. Not a sinister smile, or a sneer, or a mischievous grin, but a genuine smile . . . as if someone had given *this* Baron Von Grump a balloon, and a puppy, and a piece of cake with two scoops of ice cream and said, "Here, have this whole pitcher of fizzy soda all to yourself."

"Look at you, you handsome devil," he said to the framed picture of himself. "That was the day you finally learned to play your first complete violin song. A song *you* wrote . . ."

"Caw?" asked Edgar.

"Yes, it's quite zesty," Baron Von Grump said.

"Cawww?"

"Very lively." Baron Von Grump set the framed picture down.

"Caw caw?"

"You can certainly dance to it." Baron Von Grump tugged at his beard. "That's it, Edgar! That's exactly what I'll play. That will be the perfect song to make you feel better. Now where did I put that sheet music?"

He searched through his cabinet until he found what he was looking for.

"Eureka!" Baron Von Grump held the page of musical notes up over his head. "I found it!"

Just then the windmill tilted to the left.

Baron Von Grump stumbled. It tottered to the right. He staggered. The shutters swung open and closed. The cabinet slid this way. His stuffed chair slid that way. Baron Von Grump dropped the music and wrapped his arms around a beam to keep from sliding or falling or getting knocked over by the shifting furniture.

"What is going on?" cried Baron Von Grump.

"Caw!"

Edgar was right. The windmill paddles were out of control. They had not stopped. They had not even slowed down. They were going faster and faster. They were going so fast that they were moving the windmill this way and that!

Baron Von Grump reached out for his page of sheet music, the one with his first song on it, but a chest slid across the floor and flicked it into the air. Then a coatrack slid over and knocked the music toward the window. And then the shutters swung back and forth and pushed that music right out the window.

"NOOOOO!" said Baron Von Grump.

But it was too late. The music was gone and the windmill paddles were not slowing down.

CHAPTER
7

LAGUNA WAS HAVING A MUCH BETTER time than Baron Von Grump. She felt way better, a lot more confident, with her friends there. If they could jump into the river and learn to swim, then she could pass her swim test, she thought.

Laguna swam just like her mom had taught her, and before she knew it, she had reached the floating marker.

"I did it!" Laguna said.

Vampyra whistled. Franky clapped. Wolfy howled. They were very excited for Laguna.

"Okay, Laguna," Mrs. Lagoon said, "now swim back."

But suddenly . . .

The sky got dark. The air grew windy. And the first few drops of rain spattered down over the river.

"That does *not* look good," said Wolfy. He was looking out toward the lake, and he was right. It did *not* look good, not good at all.

All the little clouds were mashed into one big, supersized monster cloud right over the center of the lake.

"Listen to that wind!" said Vampyra.

The wind roared like a hundred—no . . . a thousand—a thousand tractor trailers rushing by on the highway. A thousand tractor trailers filled with hungry, roaring lions. And each of those lions had a bullhorn to roar through. That's how loud the wind was! Trees bent waaaaay over, their tops almost brushing the ground. And the waves! Oh, the waves . . . The water was a churning, choppy mess. It was a very good thing that Laguna, Vampyra, Franky, and Wolfy were not swimming in the lake.

"I've never seen so much rain!" Franky said. "It's all coming down over the lake."

That giant gray rain cloud was pouring so much rain on the lake that it was hard to see to the other side. No umbrella, no matter how big or how fancy, would have kept any villager dry in that rain. There was so much rain that the water was beginning to get close to overflowing, like a bathtub when the water keeps running and running and running and—

CRACK!

SLAM!

THUD!

Remember those trees that were bending over in the wind? Their tops almost brushing the ground? The roaring winds pushed two of those trees so hard that they broke right in half and fell at the mouth of the river, one after the other, piling together until they stopped most of the water from flowing.

The rain kept falling, the lake water kept rising, and now the water had nowhere to go but up. It could not flow into the river and out of the lake. It started to get deeper, and it started to trickle over the banks.

The water kept rising . . .

. . . and RISING . . .

. . . **AND RISING** . . .

"The lake is going to flood the village if we don't do something!" said Vampyra.

"We have to clear those trees!" Laguna said.

And she was right. If they could just clear those trees, the lake water could drain into the river and flow away.

"If the rain doesn't let up, I'm not so sure that anything will stop the lake from flooding the village," Mrs. Lagoon said.

Something landed in the river with a KERSPLASH!

"It's a duck!" said Franky.

"Quack."

Remember how I told you that it was so windy in the village that the ducks could not even fly? Well, that did not stop this particular duck from trying.

"Quack, quack," she said. That means *Don't worry, I'm okay.*

"Where are the rest of your friends?" Wolfy asked.

Annabelle (that was the name of this brave duck) told them all about the parade and the umbrella contest and the wind and finally . . .

"Quack quack quack quack *quack*!"

"The old windmill?" asked Wolfy.

"Out of control?" Vampyra said.

"Baron Von Grump must be behind this!" said Franky.

"We've got to stop the windmill and clear the trees that are blocking the river," said Laguna.

Mrs. Lagoon put her webbed hand out. Franky put his hand atop hers. Then Wolfy, then Franky, then Laguna, and finally Annabelle. One hand atop another (and a wing).

"Let's save the village," said Mrs. Lagoon. "I have a plan."

See? These villagers needed saving *again*. Are you surprised? Of course you

aren't. You already knew they'd have to be saved, but that's why you're reading, aren't you? To see *how* the Junior Monster Scouts will save the day. You want to see the Junior Monster Scouts in action! Well, so do I! Let's read on. . . .

8

MRS. LAGOON'S PLAN WAS A TWO-PARTER. That means there were two things they had to do. Not one thing. If it were one thing, it would be a one-part plan. This was a two-part plan, and these two things were:

- Clear the trees so that the lake did not overflow and flood the village.
- Break up the giant rain cloud so that the water stopped rising.

"It's going to take all of us to clear those trees," said Mrs. Lagoon. "Except for Vampyra."

"I want to help!" Vampyra said.

"You have a *very* important job, Vampyra," said Mrs. Lagoon.

"I do?" asked Vampyra.

"You do," Mrs. Lagoon said. "You have to fly to the windmill and try to stop it."

"But that won't make the clouds go away," said Wolfy. "They'll still be there."

Franky twisted his bolts (he did this when he was thinking) and said, "Maybe if Vampyra can make the windmill go the *other* way, it will pull the clouds back—"

"And break them up when they hit the paddles!" said Laguna.

269

"This is an excellent plan," said Mrs. Lagoon.

Vampyra did not look so sure.

"I don't know if I can fly through all that wind," she said.

Laguna put her arm around Vampyra. "You sure can! I didn't think I could swim out to the middle of the river, but you, Wolfy, and Franky gave me courage."

"Yeah, Vampyra," said Wolfy. "You can totally do it!"

"And I'll bet that's just the thing that earns you your Flying Merit Badge!" Franky said.

I know what you're thinking. . . . You're thinking, ANOTHER *merit badge?* Well, of course. What kind of scouts would they be if they were not earning merit badges? I'll bet you would like a merit badge. Perhaps you deserve a Good Reader Merit Badge? Or an Honorable Junior Monster Scout Merit Badge?

"You're right," said Vampyra.

"And we'll clear those trees," said Laguna.

"By paw or claw, by tooth or wing, Junior Monster Scouts can do anything!" Franky and Wolfy said together.

"Wish me luck," said Vampyra.

She shimmered. She shifted. And suddenly, she was a bat. A happy, flappy, little black bat.

"There she goes!" said Franky.

Wolfy cheered her on with his longest and loudest howl.

"Quack!" said Annabelle. That means *Wait . . . I'm coming with you!*

And she did. Annabelle flapped and pushed through the winds in pursuit of Vampyra.

"Now let's clear those trees," said Mrs. Lagoon.

But clearing the trees was going to be no easy task! The water was very choppy and very deep. You would have to be a strong swimmer in order to stay in that water. Franky and Wolfy were *not* strong swimmers.

But that was okay because in order to clear the trees, someone would have to stand on the shore and push while someone else stayed in the water and pulled. It was teamwork, and teamwork was something the Junior Monster Scouts were very good at.

Franky and Wolfy climbed out of the river and stood on the shore. They were going to do the pushing. Laguna and her mom stayed in the river. They were going to do the pulling.

"Laguna, this is the most challenging swim test of all," said Mrs. Lagoon. "I'd say you passed!"

Laguna grinned. Franky and Wolfy gave her a thumbs-up.

"On three," said Mrs. Lagoon. "One . . . two . . . three!"

Laguna and Mrs. Lagoon pulled the biggest tree. Franky and Wolfy pushed the biggest tree.

At first it didn't move.

Then it moved a little.

A little more.

They pulled.

They pushed.

They pulled and pushed together.

And ever so slowly . . .

The biggest tree broke free and floated downriver. With the biggest tree gone, the second broke free and floated right after it.

They'd done it! The lake was no longer blocked up. The water could flow freely down the river again.

But the rain was still pouring, and the lake was still filling up faster than it could drain. It was like running your bath on full blast when it's already filled to the top. All

that water and only one little drain for it to
go down.

Franky and Wolfy peered out toward the
old windmill.

"You can do it, Vampyra," Franky said.

Wolfy howled again.

9

VAMPYRA AND ANNABELLE FLAPPED AND fluttered and flew through the wind. It tossed them THIS way and THAT way and THIS way and THAT way.

And just when Vampyra thought that maybe she couldn't reach that old windmill, she heard a loud howl.

"Wolfy!" she said. "I'll bet Wolfy and Franky are cheering us on!"

"Quack!" said Annabelle.

"That's right," said Vampyra. "We're almost there."

Vampyra and Annabelle flew over the covered bridge. They flew over the village. They flew across the fields and straight for the old windmill. The blades were going faster and faster, and the windmill was rocking back and forth. The closer Vampyra and Annabelle flew, the stronger the wind. The stronger the wind, the harder it was to fly.

"Just . . . a . . . little . . . closer," said Vampyra. She flapped her wings as fast she could. It was almost as if she was ing in place.

But sometimes things are not that

277

Sometimes if you really want to do some-thing, you have to work a little harder than normal. And that is exactly what Vampyra and Annabelle did.

Meanwhile, inside the old windmill, Baron Von Grump held on for dear life. First the music sheets blew out the window. Then it was his plates and spoons. Then his sock collection. Then his shoes. Then the socks on his feet. Everything was blowing out the window. Even Edgar was blown right out the window!

"Cawwwwwwwwwww!!!!"

"Make. It. STOP!" cried Baron Von Grump.

Edgar snatched the rope in his beak. You remember the rope, right? The rope that

was connected to the crank? The crank that was connected to the paddles of the windmill? Well, Edgar grabbed right ahold of that rope and spun around and around and around and around with the windmill.

Poor Edgar.

"Look, Annabelle!" said Vampyra. "That's how we'll stop the windmill."

"Quack!" said Annabelle.

Vampyra and Annabelle flapped as hard as they could. They flew as fast as they could. They gritted their teeth and squinted their eyes and pushed. If they could just reach that rope!

Just . . .

. . . a little . . .

. . . bit . . .

THERE!

The rope spun around and around and around with Edgar dangling from the end. Vampyra grabbed the rope with her pointy little bat teeth. Then Annabelle grabbed the rope with her little orange duck beak.

Together, Vampyra, Annabelle, and Edgar pulled. And PULLED. And **PULLED** so hard that the windmill began to slow down. Slower. Slower. Slowwwerrrrr. Until finally, it stopped.

"Caw," said Edgar.

"Quack," said Annabelle. That means No problem.

Vampyra peered back over the lake. The big, dark rain cloud was still pouring rain.

"Okay," said Vampyra. "There's one more thing to do. Edgar, will you help us?"

Edgar squinted his eyes. He was not so sure he wanted anything more to do with this windmill.

"Caw?"

"Because the villagers are in danger," said Vampyra.

Edgar thought about this for a moment. Getting the villagers to be quiet was one thing, but being in danger was something else entirely. He certainly did not want to *hurt* the villagers, and he was sure that Baron Von Grump did not want to do that either. Besides, Edgar was tired of rain and tired of being dizzy.

Edgar shrugged. "Caw?" That means *Why not?*

"All we have to do," said Vampyra, "is make the windmill go the other way really fast. Instead of pushing the air, it will *pull* the air. That will get rid of that cloud for good. Ready?"

"Quack!"

"Caw!"

Baron Von Grump had just let go of the beam he was holding. He had just stopped being dizzy. He had just found a new pair of socks, when the old windmill started creaking and rocking and swaying again. And instead of everything blowing *out*, things were starting to blow *in*! A newspaper, a hat, an old pair of his socks . . . even a frog!

Baron Von Grump rushed to the window and looked up at the blades.

The first thing he saw was Vampyra, flittering outside his window.

"Hey there, Baron," she said, flashing him a pointy-toothed smile.

"Why, you Junior Monster Sco—"

Baron Von Grump did not finish his angry yelling. It's hard to finish your angry yelling when a frog blows right into your mouth.

"Ribbit."

THE PLAN WAS WORKING!

The faster the windmill spun in the opposite direction, the more the big, dark, stormy rain cloud was pulled away from the lake. The windmill pulled the cloud over the village. It pulled the cloud right over top of itself, where it hung for a moment, pouring down buckets of rain. Rain ran down the roof. Rain poured out of the gutters. Rain pooled around the old windmill like a castle moat, and then . . . the cloud was pulled straight through the spinning blades of the old windmill and SPLOOSH!

That big ol' rain cloud broke up into a hundred little, fluffy clouds, which drifted along like lazy lily pads. Even the sun found a nice place in the sky to stretch out its rays.

One by one, the villagers opened their doors.

"The wind is gone!" they said.

One by one, they peeked their heads out.

"The rain has stopped!" they said.

One by one, they slipped on their galoshes.

"Look at those puddles!"

And one by one, they stepped outside and jumped from puddle to puddle. (Really, what good are galoshes if you can't jump in puddles with them?)

With the storm gone, the villagers could come outside and have fun!

Vampyra and Annabelle flew back down to the village. Edgar, on the other hand, had had enough. First cranking this way and then cranking that way? His feathers were flat-out exhausted. He collapsed on the rickety roof of the old windmill, drying his feathers.

Baron Von Grump spit the frog out of his mouth.

"Ribbit!" said the frog. That means *Thank you!*

Baron Von Grump tugged at his beard. He pulled at his hair. He had a pretty good idea of who had foiled his plan. He had a pretty good idea of who was to blame for all of this mess.

He lifted his spyglass to his eye and peered out over the village. He saw exactly who he'd suspected of ruining his plan. It was that furry wolf boy, and the large one with the bolts in his neck. And that batty girl with the pointy teeth.

"Why, you Junior Monster Scouts!" he hollered. "You have foiled me for the last time!"

He shook his fist. He stomped his feet. But nobody heard him. They didn't hear one word! Not the Junior Monster Scouts, not the villagers, not even the ducks. How could they have heard anything? They were too busy splashing in puddles with their fancy galoshes. They were too busy quacking and cheering. It's hard to hear angry ranting when quacking and galoshes are involved.

No sooner had Franky and Wolfy reached the village than a bright rainbow appeared in the sky. It started from the middle of the lake, where Laguna and Mrs. Lagoon were having a celebration swim, and stretched all the way over the covered bridge, over the village, and right into the window where Baron Von Grump stood ranting.

"Oh, look," said the mayor. "The baron is waving at us. Everyone wave to the baron!"

But Baron Von Grump was not waving. Baron Von Grump was blindly trying to feel for the windowsill. The rainbow was

so bright, and so blinding, and right in his eyes. He could not see a thing! He reached this way. He reached that way. He reached too far . . . and fell out of his window, landing with a SPLASH in the giant puddles around his windmill.

"Quack," said a duck, swimming circles around Baron Von Grump.

"Ribbit," said a frog, leaping atop Baron Von Grump's head.

Baron Von Grump waved a white sock.

"I surrender," he moaned.

"OH, HELLO, JUNIOR MONSTER SCOUTS!" said the mayor. "Have you come to play in the puddles with us?"

"Actually," said Vampyra, "we were making sure everyone was okay."

"Yeah," said Franky. "Wolfy and I helped Laguna and Mrs. Lagoon clear the river so it would not flood the village."

"And Vampyra and Annabelle used the old windmill to clear the rain clouds," said Wolfy.

The mayor clapped his hands together. "Oh, splendid! Splendid, indeed! Thank you, Junior Monster Scouts! As a token of our appreciation, we, the villagers, would like to present you each with a pair of your very own galoshes!"

"Really?" said Wolfy.

"For us?" said Vampyra.

"Cool!" said Franky.

Before they left, the Junior Monster Scouts stayed for a few splashes of their own. After all, when someone gives you gift galoshes, it's quite rude *not* to make a few splashes. But then they were off, back to Castle Dracula, for that night's Junior Monster Scout meeting.

"Good-bye, villagers!" they said. "Good-bye, Annabelle. Good-bye, ducks!"

"Good-bye!" said the villagers.

"Quack!" said the ducks.

Off they marched in their new galoshes, down the road, jumping and splashing in every puddle they saw. They hopped across the covered bridge. They waded along the bank of the river and stopped to say good-bye to Laguna and Mrs. Lagoon.

"Congratulations on passing your swimming test, Laguna!" they said.

"Thank you, Junior Monster Scouts, for helping me feel brave enough and confident enough!" Laguna said.

"Come by for a swim anytime," Mrs. Lagoon said.

• • •

Franky, Wolfy, and Vampyra were so proud of their new galoshes that they wore them to that night's Junior Monster Scout meeting.

"What's with the galoshes?" said Wolf Man.

Franky, Vampyra, and Wolfy took turns telling Dracula, Wolf Man, and Frankenstein what had happened that afternoon.

"And you learned how to swim?" asked Dracula.

"You learned how to swim even though you were scared?" asked Wolf Man.

"Sounds to me like you three earned your Swimming Merit Badges," said Frankenstein. He pinned their badges onto their sashes.

"*And* your Bravery Merit Badges," said Wolf Man.

"For doing something even when you

were afraid," said Dracula. "That takes real courage."

Frankenstein pinned the Bravery Merit Badges on the Junior Monster Scouts' sashes.

"Wow," said Vampyra. "Our sashes are getting pretty full of merit badges!"

"Hope you have room for this one," said Vampyra's mom, Vampirella. She fluttered in the castle window in her bat form and then

shimmered and shifted and appeared before Vampyra in her vampire form. "You, my dear, earned your Flying Merit Badge."

"Way to go, Vampyra!" said Wolfy.

"We knew you could do it!" said Franky.

"Can I lead us in the Junior Monster Scout oath?" Vampyra asked.

"Of course," said Vampirella.

Vampyra cleared her throat and began:

"I promise to be nice, not scary."

Franky, Wolfy, and the rest of the monsters joined in.

"To help, not harm. To always try to do my best. I am a monster, but I am not mean."

Franky, Wolfy, and Vampyra recited the last line, hand in hand.

"I am a Junior Monster *Scout!*"

CHAPTER
12

BARON VON GRUMP KNEW JUST WHAT he needed to cheer himself up.

"I know just what I need to cheer myself up," he said.

See? I told you he knew. He was cold and soggy and very tired.

"A nice bubble bath," he said. "A nice, warm bubble bath will cheer me up!"

Baron Von Grump turned on the hot water. He poured in the bubbles. And while the water ran, Baron Von Grump gathered his tub things.

He gathered his robe. He gathered his slippers. He gathered a fresh towel and a long-handled scrub brush for washing his back. He gathered his bar of soap and his bath pillow and his favorite toy boat.

"Nothing like a warm bubble bath to relax," he said.

"Quack!" said a duck.

"Quack! Quack!" said two more ducks.

"Quack! Quack! Quack! Quack!" said a whole bunch of ducks.

A whole bunch of ducks swimming in Baron Von Grump's bathtub. A whole bunch of ducks playing in Baron Von Grump's bubbles.

You might say that Baron Von Grump was in a very *fowl* mood.

"Very funny. I'll bet you're just *quacking* yourself up, aren't you?"

Quack.

(That means *The End*.)

· ACKNOWLEDGMENTS ·

If you've read my acknowledgments in books 1 and 2 (*The Monster Squad* and *Crash! Bang! Boo!*), then you may recall some similarities. If you have not, you should go back and read them. There's going to be a test. A test on the content of the acknowledgments will occur in just a few short seconds. I'll wait.

Okay, good, you're back. We can start.

What is the square root of purple?

How many avocados does the Statue of Liberty weigh?

Why did the rhinoceros cross the river?

How'd you do? Feel good about it? Well, guess what? You passed! So now I can acknowledge people:

As always, I am so grateful for the love, support, and encouragement from my wife, best friend, fellow children's author, and adventuring partner, Jessica. She not only champions me and my work, but also challenges me and inspires me. Thank you, love! I'm so happy to be on this writing journey together. Like, not just a figurative journey, but a literal journey. We just bought an RV, and we're going to do some road ramblin' and coast-to-coast exploration in it!

Mad respect and admiration for my superstar editor, Karen Nagel, and the entire Aladdin team. I know you love these books as much as I do, and you've really made my vision become something even greater than I anticipated. Thank you! Karen also came up with the *perfect* titles. Much better than mine. *It's Raining Bats and Frogs!* is so much better than *Book Three*.

Thank you, Linda Epstein, for your hard work and dedication to the project. You saw it was bigger than my initial idea and encouraged me to make something more of it. I really appreciate that. Hats off to you. I'm not actually wearing a hat right now, but if I were, I would take it off. I wear a lot of hats, so I'll just wear one tomorrow and take it off to you then, okay?

Many thanks to the amazingly talented Ethan Long for his fun, zany, adorable illustrations. Wow! I just want to hug those Junior Monster Scouts! What do you say, Ethan . . . plush figures, right? Action figures? An entire line of toys . . . yeah.

As always, thanks to the modern-day Brady Bunch Jess and I have: Zachary, Ainsley, Shane,

Logan, Braeden, and Sawyer—we know you're proud of what we do. Thank you.

To our fuzzy, new puppy, Pepper . . . we love you, cute face! Even when you get the zoomies.

Thank YOU, the readers . . . because without you, there'd be no book. Or maybe there'd be a book, but no reader. And what good is a good story without a reader? If a tree falls in the forest, and nobody is around to hear it, does it still make a noise? How much wood could a woodchuck chuck if a woodchuck could chuck wood? Anyway, thanks for reading my books! And thanks for loving monsters! I hope they excite, entertain, and inspire you!

Finally, a great big thank you to all of the librarians (media specialists), teachers, and parents who battle digital distractions every day and fight to put books in the hands of young readers. Your commitment to reading, imagination, and creativity is SO important. Keep up the great work!

And thank you to the entire #kidlit community for the work that you do. The stories you write, the illustrations you do, these are the doorways to adventure that inspire the innovators of tomorrow. I am proud to stand with you.

Lastly, thank you, Sun, for vitamin D and warmth and longer days. Thank you, sharks, for not being able to come up on land. And thank you, kangaroos, for naming your babies after me: Joeys.

Monster
of Disguise

For that teacher who saw in ten-year-old me
my passion for writing and helped me believe
I could do something with it

★ ★ ★ ★

THANK YOU

CHAPTER

1

AH, SUMMER IN THE VILLAGE . . . YOU CAN practically smell the sweet scent of grass and wildflowers. Of horses and hay and freshly baked cookies. The sun is shining. The birds are singing. Boys and girls, young and old, are flying kites. All is well in the village. And why shouldn't it be? So far these villagers have managed to avoid a horde of hungry, cheese-eating rats during their annual cheese festival; celebrate their 150th birthday with only a momentary loss of power; and not get swept away by the flooding river and strong winds during a sudden spring storm.

How did they survive all of these things? I'm glad you asked. Why, the Junior Monster Scouts, of course! Those Junior Monster Scouts are always in the right place at the right time, aren't they? And speaking of Junior Monster Scouts . . . where *are* they?

Let's take a look, shall we?

Wolfy raced ahead of his cub brothers and sisters. Wolfy's dad, Wolf Man, hurled a stick over their heads.

"And . . . fetch!" Wolf Man said.

Fetch was Wolfy's favorite game. He loved running as fast as he could, jump-

ing over logs and rocks and fences, and getting that stick. Dad said he was the fastest!

"No fair!" said Wolfy's little sister Fern. "You always get the stick!"

"One of these days, I'll bet you catch me!" Wolfy said.

The rest of the cubs tumbled around Wolfy's feet, howling and barking.

Meanwhile, way up at the top of the castle tower, Vampyra gazed out her bedroom window.

"Vampyra!" Aunt Belladonna called. "Are you brushing your fangs?"

"You have to keep them shiny and pointy!" said Aunt Hemlock.

"Don't forget to floss!" Aunt Moonflower added.

Vampyra groaned and trudged back to her sink. How many times did she have to brush her fangs?

"Until they're done right!" Aunt Hemlock called up from the library.

"Reading my mind isn't fair!" said Vampyra. She stuck her toothbrush in her mouth and scowled.

Franky put the collar on his new puppy, attached her leash, and wound her up.

"Good girl!" he said. "Want to go for a walk?"

Sprocket wagged her tail. She was very excited.

"Woof!" she said. "Woof! Woof!"

Franky patted her on the head and started down the Crooked Trail. He was so excited to have a new puppy. He and his dad had made her all by themselves in Doctor Frankenstein's laboratory. Even his cousin Igor Junior had helped.

And while Franky and Sprocket walked and whistled down the Crooked Trail, while Wolfy played fetch, while Vampyra brushed her fangs *again*, and while the villagers flew kites and watched clouds, someone else was up and about. Someone with big, black, bushy eyebrows. Someone with a permanent scowl. Someone with the initials B. V. G.

Do you know who it is?

Of course you do. It was none other than Baron Von Grump.

He paced his little balcony, wringing his hands and watching the winding road that led to his crooked windmill.

"Where is it?" he asked. "It should be here this morning."

"Caw?" asked Edgar, his pet crow.

"I'm glad you asked," said Baron Von Grump. He smiled an oily, sneaky smile. The kind of smile a snake might make before it bit you. The kind of smile that makes you think someone is up to no good. "I'm waiting for a very special delivery. I have a little surprise in store for these kite-flying, cloud-gazing villagers. Every single time I try to get some peace and quiet, they have to ruin it with their noisome fun! But not this time. This time I have just the thing...."

He peered down the road. An old truck bounced and clattered toward him.

"Ah! Here it comes now!"

• • •

Oh boy, you and I know that whatever is in that truck is *not* good for the villagers, because nothing involving Baron Von Grump is *ever* good! I suppose we'll have to wait and see what it is.

FRANKY AND SPROCKET HAD ONLY JUST started down the path when Franky's mom, Esmeralda, called out to him.

"Don't forget that we're having a special scout campfire tonight!" she said.

"Oh boy!" said Franky. "Will there be s'mores?"

"S'mores and more!" she said. "But I need you to pick up some chocolate from the village. Those villagers make the best chocolate!"

It's true, you know. Imagine the best piece of chocolate you've ever had. Do you remember how sweet it was? How rich? How absolutely delicious in all of its chocolaty goodness? Now multiply that by a thousand. That's how good the village chocolate was.

Esmeralda gave Franky some money for chocolate and off he went, leash in hand and a smile on his face.

"Wait up, Franky!" said Vampyra. She flittered down from her bedroom window in bat form.

"Vampyra!" called Aunt Belladonna. "Don't forget to pick up the graham crackers for s'mores tonight!"

Vampyra wrapped her bat wings around

herself and spun in a circle. One . . . two . . .
three . . . *POOF!* She turned into herself—
shiny, brushed fangs and all.

"Hi, Vampyra!" Franky said.

"Woof!" said Sprocket. She wagged

her tail very fast. She was excited to see Vampyra.

"We're going for a walk," said Franky. "Want to come? I have to get chocolate for s'mores."

"I'm getting graham crackers," said Vampyra.

They had just reached the covered bridge when they met Wolfy. But he was not alone. He had all of his little cub brothers and sisters with him. They chased one another around his feet and nipped at his tail and howled at the sky.

"Hey, Wolfy, do you and your brothers and sisters want to come with us?" asked Vampyra.

"We have to get chocolate and graham

crackers for the s'mores tonight," said Franky.

"Me too," said Wolfy. "Mom sent us to get marshmallows . . . and exercise."

The cubs ran in circles. They leaped fallen logs. They climbed atop rocks. They had a lot of energy.

"Woof!" said Sprocket. She wanted the cubs to pet her. And, of course, they did. Who would not want to pet a puppy? A fuzzy, cute, tail-wagging puppy?

Well . . . there is *one* person who would not want to pet a puppy. There is *one* person who would look at your fuzzy, cute, tail-wagging puppy and say, *Bah! Leave me alone.* And right now, he was in his crooked windmill, opening his special delivery. . . .

• • •

"Behold!" said Baron Von Grump as he pried open the lid of the large wooden crate. "The very thing I've been waiting for!"

"Caw?" asked Edgar.

"Yes, Edgar, it is a mirror. But not just *any* mirror. This, my feathered friend, is the amazing, wondrous, spectacular, super-duper HypnoMirror! Just by gazing into this mirror, you will be hypnotized and under my control!"

Edgar covered his eyes with his wings and looked away.

"Don't worry," said Baron Von Grump. "It's not on . . . yet." And then he smiled that poisonous-snake smile, just like before.

• • •

But back in the village, things were much different. The villagers were flying kites and watching clouds and riding unicycles back and forth. There was accordion music and fresh flowers and the sweet smell of delicious chocolate.

The Junior Monster Scouts, along with Sprocket and the cubs, crossed over the covered bridge and into the village.

"I can't wait for s'mores tonight," said Vampyra. "Even if it means I have to brush my fangs a hundred more times."

"I wish I could have s'mores."

"You are," said Vampyra. She looked at Franky. "We're having them tonight, at our scout campfire, remember?"

327

"I didn't say anything," said Franky.

"A campfire? That sounds fun!"

"Wolfy, did you forget already?" Franky asked. "You know we're having a campfire. You're supposed to get the marshmallows for the s'mores."

"Of course I know," said Wolfy. "I didn't say that."

"Then who did?" asked Vampyra.

"Me."

"Me who?" asked Wolfy.

"Me who, who?"

"Are you an owl?" Franky asked, looking up at the tops of the buildings.

"No," said the voice. "I'm a boy. I'm right here!"

Franky, Wolfy, Vampyra, Sprocket, and the cubs all looked at where the voice was coming from.

But there was nobody there.

3

WHEN SOMEONE SAYS, "I'M RIGHT HERE!" and you look and there is nobody there, that can be very confusing. You might think that there is something wrong with your eyes. Or maybe that you are hearing things. Or maybe even that someone is playing a prank on you. That's exactly what the Junior Monster Scouts thought. They thought that someone was trying to play a funny trick on them.

"Peter, is that you?" asked Franky. Peter,

the piper, was a friend of the Junior Monster Scouts. They had helped him find his cat, Shadow, when she was lost in the Gloomy Woods.

"Who's Peter?" the voice asked.

"*Who* said that?" asked Wolfy.

"Where are you?" asked Vampyra. "Come out and show yourself. Stop playing tricks!"

"I'm right *here*," the voice said. "I told you guys . . ."

"Wolfy, look!" said Fern, the littlest of the little wolf cubs. She pointed to where a rock floated up off the ground and stopped. It hung in midair all by itself.

But . . . it *wasn't* all by itself. There was a hand holding it. An invisible hand that belonged to an invisible boy. Because it was invisible, nobody could see it. I'll give you an example. I'm going to tell you how this story ends, but I'm going to write it in invisible ink. Ready? Okay, just read the next line and you'll know how the story ends:

Well, what do you think? Good ending, right? Were you surprised? Wait . . . what? You couldn't read it? No, of course you couldn't read it. It was invisible. And that is exactly what the Junior Monster Scouts saw when they looked at where the rock was floating . . . nothing.

"Whoa," said Wolfy. "That rock is talking!"

"It's not the rock, it's me," said the voice. "I'm invisible!"

"That explains why we can't see you," said Franky.

"That's the problem," said the voice. "Nobody can see me. I'm just an invisible boy."

"What's your name?" asked Vampyra.

"George," said the invisible boy. "Hey, can I pet your dog?"

"You sure can, George," said Franky. "Hey, she likes you!"

Sure enough, Sprocket wagged her tail and licked the space where George must have been standing. To everyone else, it looked like she was licking the air.

"I guess that answers my question as

to why I've never seen you in the village before," Vampyra said.

"What does?" asked George.

"Being invisible," she said.

"Oh no," said George, "I don't live here. I've only just arrived. I was hoping that maybe *someone* might see me."

"It must be tough when nobody can see you," Wolfy said.

"And lonely," said George.

"My brother is a Junior Monster Scout," said Fern. She stood as tall as she could (which was not very tall at all, but she tried). "He'll help you!"

"You will?" George asked.

"Of course," said Wolfy. "We all will. That's what we do!"

"And you can even come to our camp-fire tonight," said Vampyra. "We're having s'mores!"

"Wow, thanks, Junior Monster Scouts," George said.

But the scouts did not get a chance to say "you're welcome" (which is a very nice thing to say when someone says "thanks"). Because at that moment, a very large, very colorful wagon pulled by four very large horses bounced its way up the road. It was not the wagon, or the horses, that inter-rupted their conversation. It was the man driving the large, colorful wagon, and his equally colorful cape and silly glasses and tall top hat.

"Gather round, gather round," he said,

riding his large, colorful wagon right into the middle of the village. "Stop flying your kites. Stop gazing at clouds. Put down your unicycles and gather around. Step right up, step right up, to my Fun House of . . . FUN!"

The village mayor stopped his unicycle and clapped his hands. "Ooh, that *does* sound fun!" he said.

A Fun House of Fun seems pretty awesome, doesn't it? But if the mayor had looked closer, he might have suspected that it was not going to be as fun as it sounded. If he had looked past the colorful cape, or the tall top hat, or the swirly glasses, or the striped scarf, he might have seen that the man driving this Fun House of Fun was none other than Baron

Von Grump! And Baron Von Grump is not so fun.

And had the mayor looked even closer, he might have seen a few black feathers sticking out from under that tall top hat. But he did not. Nobody did, because, well . . . Fun House of *FUN*!

"And now, simple villagers," said the top hat–wearing, cape-swirling villain in disguise, "who will be the first to step right up and have some *FUN*?" He pulled out a cane from somewhere inside of his cape, twirled it around, and pointed it at the Junior Monster Scouts. "What about you, Junior Monster Scouts?" he sneered.

But before they could answer, the mayor raised his hand. "Ooh, ooh, pick me!" he said. "I want to go first. After all, I *am* the mayor!"

Baron Von Grump smiled a crooked smile and pulled down the steps to the large wagon.

"Well then," he said, "prepare for the most fun you have ever had!"

The mayor practically skipped up the steps and opened the door to the wagon.

"Fun, here I come!" he said.

4

WHEN THE MAYOR STEPPED INTO THE wagon, he was not disappointed. The walls of the wagon were painted a very fun color. There were polka dots and stripes and swirls and splatters of rainbow colors. The floor was covered in a very fun rug. It was fuzzy and warm and had plenty of pleasing patterns. There was also some very fun music playing from a little turntable in the corner. It was the kind of music that makes you want to tap your toes and snap your fingers and bob your head to the funky beat. And while all of these things were certainly fun, what really made the Fun House of Fun *especially* fun was the peculiar mirror standing in the very center of the wagon.

The mayor stood before the mirror and made silly faces. He stuck out his tongue. He rolled his eyes. He pulled on his mustache.

"Oh my," he said, "this certainly is fun!"

But then something strange happened. Something very out of the ordinary. A large swirl formed in the middle of the mirror. It was a black-and-white swirl that began to spin, faster and faster and faster. The mayor could not look away.

And then something even stranger happened. The mayor's eyes had the exact same swirl. He was hypnotized! His swirly eyes stared straight ahead, and he shuffled out the door on the other side of the wagon.

"How was it, Mayor?" asked one villager.

"Fun," he said.

"On a scale from one to ten, how fun was it?" asked another villager.

"Fun," said the mayor.

"That sounds like the most fun ever!" said a third villager. "I'm going to buy a hundred tickets!"

"So. Much. Fun," said the mayor.

"That's right, ladies and gentle-villagers!" said the disguised Baron Von Grump. "Step right up and get your tickets here! The one and only Fun House of Fun!"

The villagers lined up, waving their money in the air. They could not wait to enter the Fun House of Fun. Why, the mayor himself had said it was So. Much. Fun.

"I'll take one," said a villager, waving her money at Baron Von Grump.

"I'll take three," said another villager, shoving his money into Baron Von Grump's hands.

"Fifteen for me!" said a third, pushing a wheelbarrow of money right up to the wagon.

"I'll have this mirror paid off in no time," Baron Von Grump whispered to Edgar.

"Caw?" asked Edgar.

"Oh yes, very expensive," said Baron Von Grump. "Terribly expensive. But it'll be worth every penny once I have them all under my control." Baron Von Grump snickered. "These villagers don't even know that they're paying for their own hypnosis!"

Baron Von Grump could not hand out tickets fast enough. Even Edgar couldn't keep up. As Baron Von Grump took the villagers' money, he handed it up to Edgar, who stashed it all under the baron's tall top hat. And as Edgar stashed the money in the tall top hat, the baron handed each villager a ticket. It read:

ADMIT ONE
FUN HOUSE OF FUN
- NO REFUNDS -

The line stretched from one end of the village to the other. Everyone wanted to have as much fun as the mayor had had. Nobody wanted to miss out. Not even Wolfy's little brothers and sisters.

"Can we go in?" asked little Fern. "Please?"

Wolfy scratched his head. He was supposed to use his money to buy marshmallows.

"Pretty puhleazzeeeee," said Fern. The

other cubs all joined in, howling and pulling at Wolfy's tail.

"Woof! Woof!" said Sprocket.

"I think Sprocket wants to go in too,"
Franky said.

"But if I buy tickets for all of the cubs,
how am I supposed to buy the marsh-
mallows for s'mores?" asked Wolfy.

"I think I can help," said George. "Since
you invited me for s'mores tonight, I
ought to bring something. What if I bring
marshmallows? And then you can use
your money to buy tickets!"

"That's a great idea," Wolfy said.

"Thank you, George!" said Fern and the
rest of the cubs. Fern would have hugged
him, but she did not know exactly where

he was standing. Being invisible made it very hard for George to be hugged.

In fact, you should stop reading for a second and hug someone you *can* see.

I'll wait. . . .

Done? Hug delivered? Okay, good. Now, where were we?

Ah, yes . . . the tickets . . .

CHAPTER
5

WOLFY STEPPED RIGHT UP TO THE MAN in the tall top hat, just like the man instructed. The man was saying, "Step right up! Step right up!" And people were! All of the villagers were stepping right up and handing the man in the tall top hat their money in exchange for a ticket into the Fun House of Fun.

"You look familiar," said Wolfy. "Do I know you?"

"Why, um . . . NO," said the man in the tall top hat (who you and I know was really Baron Von Grump in disguise). "Of course you don't. Why would you? I've never been to this village before. I don't know anything about that crooked Old Windmill, and I certainly don't live there. I'm just a simple traveler, bringing fun wherever I go. I am not up to any kind of sneaky trick, and I am certainly not wearing a disguise!"

He grinned a very toothy grin.

Wolfy shrugged. "Okay. In that case, let me have . . ." He turned to count everyone. "One, two, three . . . eleven tickets."

"But I only see ten of you," said the baron.

"That's because our friend George is invisible," said Wolfy.

"Invisible?" asked the baron. "I don't believe you."

"He's standing right there," said Wolfy. He pointed to an empty spot next to Vampyra.

"Raise your hand, invisible boy," said Baron Von Grump.

Edgar crawled out from under the top hat and peered at the spot. He didn't see anything.

"Caw!" said Edgar.

"I didn't see anyone raise a hand either," said Baron Von Grump.

"That's because he's invisible!" Franky said.

"See?" George said. "Nobody ever notices me."

"Who said that!?" asked Baron Von Grump.

"George did," said Vampyra. "We told you, he's *invisible*."

Baron Von Grump squinted one eye. He squinted the other. He peered at them very closely. He did not trust monsters, and he certainly did not trust the Junior Monster *Scouts*.

"I'm watching you," he said. "Don't think you can pull any funny tricks on me. In you go!"

Wolfy and the cubs were the first to go in.

"Wow, look at those walls!" said Wolfy. "This is fun!"

"Check out this warm, fuzzy rug!" Fern said.

"I like the music!" said another of the cubs.

"Look at this *mirror!*" said another cub.

As soon as Wolfy and the cubs were inside, the door shut behind them.

When they came out the other side, they were acting very odd.

"How was it?" asked Vampyra.

"Yeah, was it *super* fun?" Franky asked.

"It must have been SO much fun that they can't even describe it!" said George.

Wolfy and the cubs did not respond at all. It was like they were in a trance. They just stared into the clouds, and their eyes were quite strange, like swirling spirals going around and around.

"Hey, look," said Vampyra. "There's Peter. Maybe he can tell us how much fun it is."

"Peter, over here!" Franky said.

But Peter didn't answer them either. He didn't even seem to notice them. And when Franky and Vampyra looked at his eyes, they saw the same swirling spiral going around and around and around.

"I don't like this," said Vampyra.

"Something's not right," Franky said.

"Vampyra? Franky?" said George. "Look!"

They didn't have to see where he was pointing with his invisible hand to know what he was talking about.

Everyone was standing in the center of the village . . .

. . . staring at nothing with their swirling spiral eyes!

CHAPTER
6

NOW, IF YOU SAW ALL OF YOUR FRIENDS
and family staring at nothing, with swi
ing spiral eyes, you would probably sus[
that something was not right. Some[
was not right at all. This was exactly
Vampyra, Franky, and George thoug

No matter how much they t
them, no matter how many ti
waved their hands in front of
no matter how many silly fa

noises they made, nobody would even look in their direction. Not the villagers, not Peter, not even Wolfy or the cubs.

"It's like we're invisible," said Vampyra.

"Now you know how I feel," said George.

"Woof," said Sprocket. She licked George's invisible hand.

But then something even stranger happened.

The man in the tall top hat stood before the hypnotized crowd of villagers (and Wolfy and the cubs). He placed a small platform on the ground. He stepped up onto the small platform.

"Now that I have enough of you—"

"Caw," said Edgar.

"Well, most of you—"

"Caw, caw."

"Oh. Really? Well, that's even better than expected," said the man in the tall top hat to the crow sitting next to him. He turned back to the motionless villagers. "Now that I have *all* of you, it's time for a little test. Cluck like a chicken!"

The mayor, Peter, the villagers, and Wolfy and the cubs all began to cluck like chickens.

"Cluck, cluck, cluck," they all said, wiggling their arms like chickens and strutting around in circles with their heads bobbing back and forth.

It was a very funny sight to see, and Franky, Vampyra, and George wanted to laugh, but they didn't. They knew that this

top hat–wearing Fun House owner was very suspicious.

"Well, they certainly *seem* to be hypnotized," said the man in the tall top hat.

"Caw, caw, caw."

"Yes, of course, it never hurts to be sure,"

said the man in the tall top hat. "Now moo like a cow!"

As you might have guessed, all of the villagers, and the mayor, and Peter, and Wolfy and the cubs began mooing like cows. Again, it was a funny sight, but the Junior Monster Scouts were not laughing. They were very worried.

"What are they doing?" asked Vampyra.

"They're mooing," said Franky. "Like cows."

"I *know* that," said Vampyra. "I mean *why* are they mooing like cows?"

"I think they're . . . hypnotized," said George.

"Hypno-*what?*" Vampyra asked.

"You know, hypnotized," said George. "Like in a trance."

"But what could have possibly hypno-tized them?" Franky asked.

"Well, let's retrace our steps," said Vampyra. "You know, like what you do when something is lost."

"Let's start with Wolfy and the cubs," said George, "since we know everything they did before becoming hypnotized."

"They came to the village with us," said Vampyra.

"They bought tickets for the Fun House of Fun," said Franky.

"Then they went inside the Fun House of Fun," said George.

"And when they came out . . . they were hypno-sized," said Vampyra.

"Hypnotized," said George.

"That's what I said," Vampyra said.

"Aha!" said Franky. "Hypno-sized, hypno-tized . . . whatever it is, it must have something to do with the Fun House of Fun," said Franky.

"I'll bet you're right," said Vampyra. "They were normal when they went **in** and then *not* normal when they came **out**."

"There's only one way to know," said George.

"One of us is going to have to go in and check it out," said Franky.

"Not one," Vampyra said. "All of us." She put her hand out. "A Junior Monster Scout and friends . . ."

Franky put his hand on top of hers.

"... stick together till the end," he finished.

An invisible hand rested atop Franky's and Vampyra's hands.

CHAPTER
7

WHILE THE MAN IN THE TALL TOP HAT and his crow assistant performed their final test to be absolutely certain the villagers were under their complete control, Franky, Vampyra, and George were putting their tickets to use.

"Time for a little detective work," said Vampyra.

Franky opened his Junior Monster Scout

handbook and turned to the list of merit badges. "You know," he said, "I'll bet we can even get our Mystery Merit Badges if we solve this case."

"I think you're right," said Vampyra. "This sure sounds like a mystery to me!"

Franky, Vampyra, and George placed their tickets in the ticket box and climbed up the steps and through the door of the Fun House of Fun. Sprocket waited outside.

The inside was, as you and I know, very fun. There was fun music playing, fun rugs on the ground, fun paint on the walls, and a very, *very* fun mirror right in the middle of the room.

"Haha," said Franky. "I look super tall. The mirror stretched me out!"

"Look at me," said Vampyra. "I look shorter and kind of flat!"

"Aw, rats," said George. "I don't see anything at all."

"Did someone say 'rats'?" said a very large rat, gnawing on a hunk of cheese.

That was Boris, and he lived in the basement of Castle Dracula with all of the other rats. They were always sticking their cheese-covered noses into everyone's business. Boris was not alone. There were several other rats with him.

But it was a good thing that Boris and the rats *did* stick their cheese-covered noses into this business because just as the Junior Monster Scouts were staring at the mirror, their eyes began to turn swirly and spiral and lose all focus. . . .

"Hey! Junior Monster Scouts," said Boris the rat. "We're talking to you. Over here! Wow . . . that's a *fun* mirror!"

Vampyra, Franky, and George heard Boris and turned from the mirror just in time.

"Boris, what are you doing here?" asked Vampyra.

"Hey, look at their eyes!" Franky said.

"They're swirly spirals, just like everyone's outside!" George said

Sure enough, Boris and the rats weren't eating their cheese anymore, and Boris didn't answer Vampyra's question. It wasn't because they were being rude—it was because they were hypnotized!

Have you ever been hypnotized? No? I want you to do something. On the count of three, I want you to quack like a duck. Do you know how to quack like a duck? I'll bet you do. Okay, ready? One . . . two . . . three!

Ah, very good. But guess what? I just

hypnotized you! I made you quack like a duck. That was exactly what was happening to Boris and the rats, and Wolfy and the cubs, and Peter, the mayor, the villagers . . . Wow, that is a lot of quacking and mooing and clucking and barking. That is a lot of noise.

And do you know who doesn't like noise?

Baron Von Grump.

Which is why, at that exact moment, he made everyone *stop* making animal noises. No more quacking. No more mooing. No more clucking or barking. He made everyone be quiet.

"Silence!" he said.

Everyone was absolutely silent.

He took off his tall top hat and removed the rest of his disguise.

"Ah, do you hear that, Edgar?" he asked.

"Caw?" Edgar asked.

"Exactly," said Baron Von Grump. "There's nothing to hear. Nothing! Because finally,

the day has come. Finally, the villagers are quiet. No gum chewing, no smiling, no accordions or 'Hello, how do you do?' No walking, no talking, no singing or kite flying. Absolute silence.

"This," said Baron Von Grump, "is the moment I've been waiting for."

He closed his eyes and smiled.

It was an awkward smile. Like maybe a quarter of a smile. He really wasn't any good at smiling, but hey, he tried.

"Edgar?"

"Caw?"

"Breathe quieter."

CHAPTER
8

INSIDE THE FUN HOUSE OF FUN, THE Junior Monster Scouts and George had just discovered something. Something very important. Something that could help them solve this mystery.

"I think it has something to do with the mirror," said Franky.

"When I was looking at the mirror, I began to feel a little sleepy," said Vampyra.

"Me too," said Franky.

"I didn't feel a thing," said George. "This place really isn't that fun. I couldn't even see myself in the mirror."

"And when Boris and the rats looked in the mirror, *they* became hypno-sized!" Vampyra said.

"Hypnoti*zed*," said George.

"That's what I said."

"That's it!" said Franky. "When someone sees themself in the mirror, they become hypnotized."

"Just like Boris and the rats," said Vampyra. "Hey, where are they going?"

Boris and the rats all walked in a quiet single-file line, right through the other

door and out of the Fun House of Fun. They weren't even eating their cheese. That's how quiet they were being!

"Come on," said Vampyra. "Let's follow them!"

Franky, Vampyra, and George followed Boris and the rats. They followed them right to the center of the village, where everyone stood in a trance, watching someone sitting atop a hay wagon.

That someone was enjoying every second of his newly created silence.

That someone was Baron Von Grump.

"Oh, what a glorious day," he said. "Oh, wonderful, magnificent, *quiet* day!"

"It's Baron Von Grump!" said Vampyra.

"Caw?" asked Edgar, turning in their direction.

Franky and Vampyra ducked. George did not duck in time.

But as you might have guessed, Edgar did not see him.

"It's nothing," said Baron Von Grump. "There's no one there. See?" He pointed in their direction, and sure enough, there was nobody to be seen.

Edgar shrugged.

The Junior Monster Scouts breathed a sigh of relief.

George had an idea.

CHAPTER
9

GEORGE'S IDEA WAS A VERY GOOD IDEA. He and the Junior Monster Scouts had figured out that the mirror had something to do with everyone being hypnotized. They also knew that only Franky and Vampyra could see their reflections in the mirror, which meant . . .

"If I can't see myself in the mirror, and nobody else can see me, then I'll bet I won't get hypnotized!" said George.

"You're right!" Franky said.

"Brilliant!" said Vampyra. "Don't worry, Wolfy. Don't worry, cubs. We're going to unhypno-size you!"

But Wolfy and the cubs did not respond.

George did not bother to try to correct her this time. "I thought vampires couldn't see their reflections in the mirror," he said.

Vampyra shrugged. "That's just another made-up story. Okay, what now?"

"Follow me," said George.

"George?" said Vampyra.

"Yes?"

"We can't."

"Oh, right," he said. "Invisible. You go inside first."

Vampyra went first. Then Franky. He told Sprocket to wait outside.

"Bark twice if anyone comes, okay?"

Sprocket wagged her tail and sat by the door. She was a very good watchdog.

George followed them inside the Fun House of Fun and shut the door.

"Now what?" asked Vampyra. She was very careful to keep her eyes off the mirror.

"We need something to cover the mirror with," said George.

Franky had an idea. He reached outside and snatched Baron Von Grump's cape from the hook on the wagon.

"We can use this," he said. He was also very careful to keep his eyes off the mirror.

"Good thinking!" said George.

"Okay, George," said Vampyra. "Cover that mirror!"

George stood in front of the mirror. He looked right into it. All he saw was a cape, floating in the air. George stepped closer and covered the mirror with the cape.

Outside, Baron Von Grump sat atop a mound of hay, in the back of a wagon, in the center of the village, in complete and utter silence. He closed his eyes.

He took a deep breath. It . . . was . . . perfect.

"Caw?" Edgar asked.

Baron Von Grump glowered at Edgar.

"I don't know where those other monsters are, and I don't care," he said. "Can't you see I finally have my moment of silence?"

"Caw," said Edgar. He pointed back to the Fun House of Fun.

"Yes, yes, they may be in the Fun House of Fun. But who cares? They'll be hypnotized just like everyone else!"

Edgar shrugged.

"Now, silence!" said Baron Von Grump.

He closed his eyes. He took a deep breath. He listened to . . . nothing.

Silence

Shhhhh . . . .

Quiet zone

No talking

This means you!

Don't read this aloud.

Too late . . . You're already doing it?

Well, stop.

What do you mean you can't stop?

Do you *have* to read the words on the page?

What do you mean,

"That's what the words on the page are for"?

Fine, be that way.

CHAPTER
10

"LOOK, THERE'S A LEVER," SAID FRANKY.

Vampyra groaned. "Oh no, not another lever," she said.

Vampyra, Franky, and Wolfy had had a very scary experience with a lever in Doctor Frankenstein's laboratory when they'd helped their friend Igor Junior get out of trouble.

"I think this one is okay," Franky said.

"How do you know it's okay?" Vampyra asked.

"It could do anything!" said George.

"There has to be a way to turn it on and off, right?" Franky asked.

"And there doesn't appear to be any other buttons, switches, or levers," said George.

"Wait . . . there's writing," said Franky.

"What's it say?" asked Vampyra.

Franky peered closer. "It says . . ."

HYPNOTIZE

OFF

REVERSE

"So all we have to do is move the lever to reverse," said George.

"Here goes nothing," Franky said.

He pulled the lever.

Baron Von Grump had just settled into a calm, quiet, relaxed moment of silence when . . .

"Woof!" said Sprocket.

Baron Von Grump jumped. He was not expecting Sprocket to bark, and it startled him. But Sprocket was not barking to startle him. She was barking because Wolfy and the cubs had snapped out of their hypnosis. Their eyes weren't spirals or swirly. They seemed very confused. Everyone seemed very confused.

"Sprocket!" Wolfy said. "Where're Franky and Vampyra? Wait a minute. . . . Baron Von Grump?"

"What's going on here?" asked the mayor.

"Why are we all out here around this wagon?" asked another villager.

"Say, what are you doing up there on my hay?" asked a third villager.

"I can explain!" said Baron Von Grump. "It . . . It wasn't me. It was . . ."

"Caw!" said Edgar. "Caw! Caw!"

"Yes, exactly. It was another guy with a very tall top hat, and funny glasses, and a colorful scarf. He hypnotized you! I was just trying to break the spell!"

Wolfy sniffed the air. It smelled like Baron Von Grump was not telling the truth.

"You mean this very tall top hat?" Fern asked. She and the other cubs appeared from behind the ticket stand carrying one very tall top hat.

"And *this* colorful scarf?" asked another cub.

"And these funny glasses?" asked a third cub.

"How did those get there?" asked Baron Von Grump. "Haha . . . that's strange, isn't it?"

"Not as strange as that mirror inside the Fun House of Fun," said a voice right next to Baron Von Grump.

"Who said that?" asked Baron Von Grump.

You and I and Wolfy and the cubs know who said it, but nobody else did because they could not see him. But George had climbed right up next to Baron Von Grump.

"Who said what?" George asked.

"Who's talking?" asked Baron Von Grump. "Who's playing tricks on me?"

"You mean tricks like . . . *hypno-sizing people?*" asked Vampyra. She flittered over to the wagon in her bat form.

"And making them cluck like chickens and moo like cows?" Franky asked. He carried the large, cape-covered mirror out of the Fun House of Fun and set it down.

"Explain yourself," said the mayor.

"I want my money back!" said a villager.

"Get off my hay!" said another villager.

"You wouldn't happen to have any cheese, would you?" Boris asked.

"Caw!" said Edgar.

"Yes!" said Baron Von Grump. "Run!"

He jumped down from the hay wagon and ran as fast as he could toward the Old Windmill. Edgar flapped along above him.

"You can't stop Baron Von Grump forever, you meddling monsters!" he hollered.

"I think your village may have seen the last of him for a bit," said a floating tall top hat and a pair of funny glasses.

"Oh my!" said the mayor. "A talking top hat!"

"George!" Vampyra said. "We can really see you now! Kind of."

"Oh yeah?" he said. "Well, check this out. . . ."

He pulled the cape off the mirror.

Everyone gasped and closed their eyes tight.

CHAPTER
11

"IT'S OKAY," GEORGE SAID. "YOU CAN open your eyes."

When the Junior Monster Scouts and the villagers opened their eyes, they saw an ordinary mirror. And standing in front of the mirror was *not* an ordinary sight.

"That cape is floating!" said a villager.

"Just like those silly glasses!" said another.

"And that very tall top hat!" a third vil-lager said.

"No, they're not," said Vampyra. "George is wearing them."

"Who's George?" the mayor asked.

"He's our friend," said Franky.

"He's indivisible," said Fern.

"She means *invisible*," Wolfy said.

Fern shrugged. "That's what I said."

George was very pleased that everyone could, kind of, finally see him. It was nice to be noticed for once.

"George helped us turn off Baron Von Grump's hypnotic mirror," Vampyra said.

"If it weren't for George's help, we might all be hypnotized still," said Franky.

"Moo!" Wolfy said.

Everyone laughed.

"Well," said the mayor, "I think we can find you a better set of clothes than a cape and a very tall top hat. Come with me, young George."

"Where are we going?" George asked.

"Why, to the tailor, of course," said the mayor. "We'll have you dressed in a whole new outfit so that wherever you go in the village, people can stop and say, 'Good morning, George!' and 'How do you do?'"

If Baron Von Grump had heard that, he would have had a fit. Another person in the village to go around saying "good morning"? He would not like that at all.

Speaking of Baron Von Grump . . .

CHAPTER
12

BARON VON GRUMP FUMED. HE FUSSED. He tugged his beard and pounded his fists.

"It was all so perfect!" he said. "It was all going according to plan!"

"Caw! Caw! Caw!" Edgar said.

"Well, how was I to know that those Junior Monster Scouts had an invisible friend? Whose side are you on, anyway?"

Edgar crossed his wings and shook his

head. Sometimes living with Baron Von Grump was a very trying experience. Okay, most of the time. All right, probably *all* of the time.

Just then, there was a knock at the front door.

CHAPTER 13

WHILE GEORGE WAS GETTING FITTED at the tailor's, the Junior Monster Scouts busied themselves getting everything they needed for the s'mores. Franky bought the chocolate. Vampyra bought the graham crackers. All they needed were the marsh-mallows.

"Hi, Junior Monster Scouts!" George said.

"Hi, George!" they replied. They could see him now because he was dressed in a whole new outfit. He had a pair of buckled shoes and knee-high socks, pants and a shirt, gloves and glasses, and even a fancy cap on his head. A fancy cap with a feather! The only things they could not see were his mouth and nose.

"I never thought that new clothes might make a difference," he said. "My old clothes must have turned invisible in the same experiment that first turned *me* invisible."

He was also holding a bag of marsh-mallows.

"Brought you these," he said.

"Now we can have s'mores tonight!" said Fern.

The other cubs all howled with delight.

Sprocket barked and howled along with them.

"Ah, there you are," said the mayor. "George, you are looking splendid. Simply magnificent! I want to show you all something."

The mayor led them to the village square where Peter, the piper, stood next to something tall and rectangular and covered with a sheet.

Peter pulled the sheet off to reveal a full-length mirror. Only, when you looked at it, you did not get hypnotized. Instead, it made you look squashed and extra wide, or stretched out and super skinny, or wavy and wobbly. It was a new fun-house mirror, and this one was actually FUN!

"Junior Monster Scouts, George," said the mayor, "you taught us all another valuable lesson today. It's not what you look like—it's what you *do*. We used to be scared of the monsters because they looked different, but they always come to our aid. And George, you weren't noticed because of what you looked like . . . or *didn't* look like . . . but because you helped save us all from being hypnotized!"

"So what's the mirror for?" asked Wolfy. He stuck his tongue out, and his reflection looked even sillier. His tongue looked ten times as long!

"Because when we look into it," Peter said, "we're reminded that things aren't really what they seem! Even if it *looks* that way."

"But where did that hypnotizing mirror go?" Franky asked.

"You know," said the mayor, "I really don't have the slightest idea."

CHAPTER
14

REMEMBER THAT KNOCK AT THE FRONT door of the Old Windmill?

"I'm coming!" hollered Baron Von Grump. "Quit pounding on my door! Noise, noise, noise, NOISE. Always with the noise. What do you—"

"Hey, Von Grump," said Boris the rat. "You left this back at the village. Figured you might want it back."

Baron Von Grump's eyes got very wide.

The rats had brought him back his mirror. His hypnotic mirror.

And they'd just pushed the lever to HYPNOTIZE.

Baron Von Grump's eyes became spirals. Then they got swirly. He was very sleepy.

"Cluck like a chicken," said Boris.

"Cluck! Cluck!" said Baron Von Grump.

"Oink like a pig," said another rat.

"Oink, oink, oink!" Baron Von Grump said.

"Come on," said Boris, leading the rats into the Old Windmill, "let's grab some cheese and sit back and watch the show!"

"Oink, oink, oink!" said Baron Von Grump.

Edgar covered his ears with his wings. Baron Von Grump was SO *noisy!*

CHAPTER

15

THAT NIGHT'S SCOUT MEETING TOOK place around a nice, toasty campfire. Can you smell the wood burning? Can you hear the crackle? Can you see the bright embers dancing up into the star-filled summer sky? Campfires are nice. Summer campfires are even nicer. And summer campfires with s'mores? The best.

"Well, sounds like you had a very exciting afternoon," said Esmeralda. She handed out marshmallow sticks. There were a lot of sticks. Not only were the Junior Monster Scouts there; and their moms; and Vampyra's aunts Belladonna, Hemlock, and Moonflower; but also Dracula, and Wolf Man, and Doctor Frankenstein, and the cubs, and Sprocket, and Igor Junior, and Igor Senior, and finally, last but certainly not least, George.

Wolfy's mom, Harriet, opened her Junior Monster Scout handbook. "Let's start tonight's meeting by saying the scout oath," she said. Everyone joined in.

"*I promise to be nice, not scary. To help, not harm. To always try to do my best. I am a monster, but I am not mean. I am a Junior Monster Scout!*"

"It sounds like you weren't only helpful

today," said Vampyra's mom, Vampirella. "It sounds like you were clever."

"Regular detectives!" said Aunt Belladonna.

"Supersleuths!" said Aunt Hemlock.

"No clue too confusing for these clever monsters!" Aunt Moonflower said.

"Which is why you are receiving your Mystery Merit Badges," said Harriet. "All four of you."

She looked right at George and pinned the merit badge to his shirt.

George smiled, and even though no one could *see* his smile, they could *feel* it.

"Gee, thanks!" he said.

"You're very welcome," said Esmeralda.

"I believe we have another surprise tonight, don't we?" said Dracula.

Vampirella smiled. Her fangs glinted in the campfire light.

"Indeed we do," she said. "Fern, cubs, congratulations. You are the very first *Little Junior Monster Scouts!*"

Wolfy leaped up and howled at the moon. Everyone howled along with him.

It was a Junior Monster Scout meeting to remember!

OINK!

CLUCK!

MOO!

· ACKNOWLEDGMENTS ·

Wow . . . here we are, at the end of the fourth book in the Junior Monster Scouts series. It goes without saying that I want to thank my amazing wife, Jess (not that I have other wives, but I thought it'd be nice to mention her name and not just call her "my wife," and if I'd thanked "Jess," you might have asked, "Who's Jess?"), for her love, support, encouragement, inspiration, and friendship. I want to thank my editor, Karen Nagel, for opening this door to me in the first place and for championing these books. Karen, you and the Aladdin team made these books even greater than I could have ever imagined them. Chelsea

Morgan, thanks for putting up with my habitual mistake with a certain dialogue tag. Thank you, Linda Epstein, for all of the hard work you have done (and continue to do) with this series. Thank you, Ethan, for your wonderful illustrations. I'm a lucky author to be partnered with you.

Shane, Zach, Logan, Ainsley, Sawyer, and Braeden—thank you for being proud of what we do. We are proud of each one of you. And by "we" I am, of course, referring to Jess and to myself, and not speaking about myself only in some strange third-person kind of reference. Thank you, Becca, Josh, Madi, and Lena, for being you.

I recently attended a book festival, and someone asked me what it felt like, or

414

what my reaction was, to holding my first published book in my hands. My first book was published in 2015, and I'm fortunate to have quite a few books out now and even more on the horizon, but my answer was this: it was a surreal and wonderful feeling of accomplishment to know that I'd done what I set out to do when I was a ten-year-old with a dream—to hold in my hands a book that an agent, an editor, and you, the reader, felt was important enough, fun enough, good enough to invest in. And, I continued to say, that has never changed. I get that same feeling with every book. I am grateful for every opportunity, every reader, every book I publish. I am reminded of what I have managed to do and to not take any of this for granted. I am truly thankful for the ability and opportunity to put these books in your hands.

And speaking of book festivals, thank you so much to every organizer and volunteer of every book festival out there. Your hard work presents so many opportunities for us (the authors and illustrators) to meet old and new readers and share our art. Thank you, independent bookstore owners, for being the beating heart of the book world. There's so much more to this gig than shelf space and ISBNs.

Thank you to the teachers and librarians who celebrate reading, creativity, art, and writing in a STEM world. The classroom libraries you build, the book fairs, the authors and illustrators you bring in, and the school-wide reading nights may be more important to a young person than you may realize (but I'm betting I'm wrong—I'm betting you know just how important it is). And trust me when I say that you are making a difference. You may never know it, but you are. I might not ever learn the name of the fourth-grade teacher who changed my life. (We moved so much that it was somehow lost in the shuffle.) I will most likely never get a chance to thank her personally. But she saw in me what you see in some of your students, and her encouragement and belief in my potential put me on a trajectory that has me sitting here typing acknowledgments in this book. I am the fruit of your labor, teachers.

Lastly, I want to thank all of my fellow children's writers and illustrators. The art you produce, the work you do (from the books to the school visits to the signings and festivals), is a bright light in a sometimes dark world. We are the torchbearers. We bring the magic. I'm very proud to stand with you, helping children to learn, laugh, love, and discover. Yes, I know . . . discover does not start with an "l," and I missed a chance at nailing a four-word alliteration. But seriously, thank you. We all lift one another up and propel each other forward. Our kidlit community is pretty amazing.

Finally (even though I just previously said "lastly"), I'd like to thank every mom and dad who takes their kids to the bookstore and the library, who sends in their Scholastic Book Club money, who says yes to buying another book. I'm not thanking you for your money (although yes, I am thankful for that—it'd be rude not to say thanks for that, don't you think?)—I'm thanking you for feeding a child's hungry imagination, curious creativity, and insatiable appetite to explore new worlds and delve into new adventures. Thank you for saying yes when it's just as easy to say no.

Best to you all!

Joe

JOE McGEE loves to write about monsters and magic and other strange, curious, and quirky things. He grew up with his nose in a book and his imagination exploring other worlds. He knew when he was ten years old that one day he would grow up to be an author! He has an MFA in Writing for Children and Young Adults from the Vermont College of Fine Arts and a Master of Arts in Writing from Rowan University. Joe teaches at Sierra Nevada University's low-residency MFA program and teaches English at Eastern West Virginia Community and Technical College. He is a former army officer and lives in the mountains of West Virginia with his wife (also a children's author), Jessica Rinker. Visit JoeMcGeeAuthor.com to learn more about Joe and his books.